FIRST LOVE

A SECOND CHANCE ROMANCE

Hazel Kelly is the author of several romance novels.
She was born in the United States and lives in Ireland.

D1736641

FIRST LOVE

A SECOND CHANCE ROMANCE

Hazel Kelly

First published 2016.

ISBN-13: 978-1539605416

Printed and bound by CreateSpace.

Cover Artwork – © 2016 L.J. Anderson of Mayhem Cover Creations

If you love something, let it go.

If it comes back to you, its yours forever.

If it doesn't, then it was never meant to be.

- Anonymous

Prologue

They say you'll never forget your first love, and that's definitely true in my case.

I think that's because he was my first everything. My first crush, my first kiss, my first… home run.

I don't know what it was about Adam, but from the moment I met him, being around him wasn't just a cerebral stimulant. It was a full body experience.

Perhaps it was because he seemed foreign compared to the kids I grew up with or maybe it was his magnetic confidence.

Whatever it was, his instant interest in me made me feel special, as if I were more than the regular girl I believed myself to be before I first heard my name on his lips.

Unfortunately, the only predictable thing about our relationship- if you could even call it that- was that we never seemed to have enough time together.

On the one hand, that was a blessing. It meant I never had to deal with the pain of watching the spark between us fizzle as we grew up and grew apart.

Then again, maybe it wouldn't have. Maybe it would've ignited further and turned into something... more.

Not that it mattered.

The past was the past.

And even though I might've preferred the risk of getting temporarily hurt to the permanence of never knowing- to the loose ends and the unfinished business and all the unasked questions- I needed to put my teenage daydreams behind me.

Sure, I'd always cherish the memories from that summer our childhood fascination with each other matured into life affirming intimacy, but I needed to move on and accept the fact that I'd never see him again.

Though part of me refused to give up hope.

But like a candle, hope can only burn for so long, and mine had nearly flickered out.

After all, so many years had passed since I'd seen him that my perfect summer crush had become nothing but a string of scattered, faded flashbacks that seemed too good to be true and too old to keep on such a dusty pedestal.

Of course, as soon as I was ready to forgive and forget, he walked back into my life out of the blue- sexier, bolder, and more unattainable than ever.

And as if invigorated by a gust of warm ocean breeze, my candle burned bright again.

ONE
- Jolie -

I clipped my thin gold name tag to my crisp white shirt, checked to make sure I didn't have any lipstick on my teeth, and flicked off the lights in my apartment.

Then I descended the stairs into the backyard and opened the door to my mom's house. "Good morning," I said, inhaling the glorious scent of the freshly brewed coffee beans I'd come for.

"Perfect timing," she said, filling two mugs without turning around.

I pulled out a chair at the small round table and took a seat. "How did you sleep?"

She made her way over in her short yellow robe. "Lying down," she said, setting our favorite Winnie the Pooh mugs on some coasters.

"I should try that sometime."

She furrowed her thin brows, her face pale without makeup. "Tell me you didn't fall asleep on the couch again?"

I shrugged. "What can I say? It's a comfortable couch."

"You're working too hard," she said, shaking her head as she sat down.

I slid my mug towards me, wondering why people got so excited about coffee shops. As far as I was concerned, coffee was best enjoyed out of a favorite mug at home. Bringing lines and ordering and money into the exchange only ruined the otherwise peaceful morning ritual.

"I blame myself," she said.

"Don't. It's good that we're busy."

"Not busy enough," she said.

I furrowed my brow. "What are you talking about? We literally ran out of margarita mix yesterday."

"A hotel like ours shouldn't run out of margarita mix at the height of summer," she said. "We shouldn't even be buying margarita mix."

I squinted at her. "Are you sure you slept okay?"

"The fact that we ran out is down to budget cuts, not a surge of customers."

"What do you mean budget cuts?" I asked.

She sighed and looked down at the steam rising from her mug.

"Why the long face, Mom? It's not a big deal."

"I know," she said. "But what I'm about to tell you is."

My eyes grew wide. "Are you okay? You're really freaking me out."

"As of today, the hotel is officially under new management."

The hair on the back of my neck stood up. "What are you talking about? I'm the manage-"

"I sold it. To a developer."

My throat closed up.

She kept her sad eyes on me.

I shook my head. "I don't understand. What do you mean you sold it?"

"Someone made me an offer a few weeks ago, and I decided to take it."

I craned my neck forward. "How could you not discuss this with me? I've given up everything for this place!"

"I had no choice."

I splayed my hands on the table. "Of course you had a choice!"

"We've been losing money ever since your father died, and I didn't want to run his legacy into the ground."

"So you sold it?!"

"It was going to kill me," she said, her shoulders sagging. "Just like it killed your father."

The coffee taste on my tongue turned bitter. "Look, I know you've resented the place since dad died, but it was his baby- his dream- and that feeling will pass." I leaned forward. "We can make it great again. That's what he would want."

"I can't." She shook her head. "There's no money, and I don't have the energy or the expertise to save it, much less take it to the next level."

I sat back. "You're serious."

"I'm afraid so."

"I thought we were doing okay."

She pressed her lips together. "I may have fudged the truth a bit so I wouldn't worry you."

"So that's it? Everything you and dad worked so hard for amounts to nothing but a payout?"

"Of course not."

I clenched my jaw. "I find that hard to believe if you could just give it away."

"I didn't give it away," she said, her voice taking on new strength. "I sold it to someone who wants to make it great again, someone with a passion for the place that I no longer have."

"How could you do this to me?"

"I'm not doing it to you." She dropped her chin. "I'm doing it for you."

I threw my hands in the air. "That's bullshit. The hotel was all we had left. It was supposed to secure our future."

"I'm still hoping it will," she said. "Now that it will actually have one."

I covered my face.

"The man I sold it to really understands the hotel's potential. His family used to be regular customers of ours when you were little."

I dropped my hands and furrowed my brow. "What kind of loyal customer takes someone's business away?!"

"He didn't take it."

"Oh right. Because you gave it to him."

"He's going to save the business, Jolie. That's why I brought him on board."

"You don't get it. He's going to have no respect for how we do things, how we've always done things."

"Of course he will," she said, wrapping her hands around her mug. "I wouldn't have sold it to him if I didn't think he understood our vision for the place."

"What vision?!" I asked, sliding my chair back. "Vision is something you have when you plan on sticking around to see something through, and it looks to me like you're checking out and leaving the rest of us there with a stranger who didn't even know dad!"

"It's what your father would've wanted."

"It's what you want." I stood up. "And only you."

"Please calm down, Jo. I need you to support me on this."

"Obviously you don't," I said, lifting my purse off the back of the chair. "Or you would've talked to me about it before you signed Dad's dream away."

"Please don't go to work upset," she said, laying her hands on the table. "The rest of the staff is going to look to you for how to take the news. If you can't hold it together, the whole deal is going to fall apart."

I scoffed. "And here I thought you were worried about my stress levels."

"I am, honey. I promise things are going to get better because of this."

"You can't promise shit right now," I said, slinging my purse across my body. "We won't have any control of the resort going forward. You effectively made me an employee."

"You can learn a lot from this man."

"Like what? How to take what isn't mine?" I picked up my mug, walked over to the sink, and poured my coffee down the drain.

"No," she said, standing. "Like how to take a struggling business and turn it into a profitable one."

I marched to the door, my heels tapping on the linoleum tiles. "I hope that's what happens for Dad's sake," I said, opening the door.

She pulled her robe tight. "I'm sorry, honey."

"No you're not," I said, struggling to keep my voice from shaking. "You're selfish."

"It was the only way I could secure our future."

I shook my head. "Your future. It was the only way you could secure *your* future."

She sighed. "I understand that you're upset, but please be strong for the staff. I'm counting on you to make them see that this is a good thing."

"I'm a hotel manager, Mom, not a magician," I said, closing the door behind me, my heart aching with the knowledge that my father's life's work had been sold to the highest- no- the only bidder.

"May Dad forgive you," I mumbled as I headed down the driveway. "Because that's more than you can expect from me."

TWO

- Adam -

"So?" I asked, dragging a french fry through some ketchup. "What do you think?"

"I think it's an interesting choice," Ben said, leaning back.

"Were there really no words that came to mind before interesting? That's got to be the least supportive thing you could have said."

Ben reached for his lemonade and drank from his straw as his eyes travelled the length of the Harmony Bay Resort Hotel. "It needs a lot of work."

"So did your warehouse, if my memory serves."

"Yeah, but that was a blank slate," he said. "This is…"

First Love

I raised my eyebrows.

"A messy, dated slate."

"So it needs some updating to be a five star resort. I get that." I popped another fry in my mouth. "That's why I got it for such a steal."

"Don't get me wrong. It has potential. I just think it's going to take a lot more work than you realize."

"I don't mind a challenge," I said, raising a finger towards him. "And just you wait. It'll be so nice you'll want to open one of your clubs down the street."

Ben laughed so hard his eyes watered from the lemonade he coughed up his nose.

"Now you're just being a dick."

"Sorry." He shook his head and raised a palm at me. "I didn't mean to be unsupportive. I just think you're kidding yourself if you think you're going to be able to give this place that much of a facelift."

I raised my eyebrows. "Do you have anything nice to say about the place?"

He scrunched his face. "Everything's really cheap?"

"I know," I said. "Too cheap."

"So that's good," he said.

"Because you think it'll be profitable?"

"Oh definitely," he said. "In a few weeks' time- after you've done some of the most urgent renovations- I think you'll be able to double the price of everything."

I nodded. "That's promising."

"Even this lemonade," he said, holding it up. "I thought it was going to taste like shit for how cheap it is, but it's actually delicious. Same with my burger."

"Careful now. That's two nice things. I wouldn't want you to actually be supportive."

He leaned back in his patio chair. "Sorry, bud. My imagination just isn't active enough to understand why- of all the places you could invest your money- you'd pick this place."

"Because it was important to me growing up," I said, shrugging. "I have such great memories of being a kid here. Plus, hooking families up with a nice holiday is a new challenge for me."

"Are you sure you're not just mixing business and pleasure?" he asked.

I scoffed. "As if you don't approve. You literally built a club so you could hang out with beautiful women and put fancy gin cocktails on your expenses."

"No. I built the club because I wanted to be in the entertainment industry and-"

"You have no genuine talent?"

"Ouch."

I dragged my napkin across my mouth. "The point is, I don't have to have a family to build the best family resort in the southeast."

"If you say so."

"I do," I said. "If anything, it's probably an advantage to not have the distraction."

He looked towards the pool before letting his eyes travel up to the top of the water slide where a short line of kids were egging each other on.

I crumpled my napkin and shoved it under the edge of my plate. "Maybe if you're nice, I'll hook you and Carrie up with a sick room for you and your Abbott offspring someday."

"You'll have to make a competitive offer," he said. "We get some pretty good deals at my dad's hotels."

"Speaking of which- since your dad basically wrote the book on the hospitality business- what concerns would he have if he were here?"

Ben twisted his mouth. "I think he'd be worried about how seasonal the business is," he said, folding his hands in his lap. "Do you have any idea how quiet this place gets in the off season?"

I nodded. "It does get quiet, but I'm cool with that. It's only meant to be a side project, and it's easier to oversee something that doesn't need year round coddling."

"True, but you've got a much shorter money making window here than you do with the backpacking tour business."

I leaned back and glanced at the families enjoying their lunches on the deck around us, knowing full well that at least fifty percent of them would probably come here every summer until their kids didn't feel like vacationing with them anymore. Of course, making the place more attractive to older kids was just one of the improvements I intended to make.

Plus, the pace of life was so free and easy here compared to where I grew up on the Upper East Side. I liked the idea that I might vacation here with my own family someday, that my kids would know how to fly kites and catch waves and build sand castles.

"I think I can turn the place around one season at a time," I said. "And if it's even half as successful as the backpacker tours, I'll be laughing."

"I hope you're right," Ben said.

"What does Carrie think?"

"Carrie thinks the place needs updating, but she looks at things differently than I do."

I raised my eyebrows.

"She's already full of ideas for how you can modernize the rooms and the common areas."

"So she'll help?" I asked.

"Absolutely. She's never done a hotel before. She's thrilled that you thought of her."

"Of course."

"And she thinks the local area is the cutest place she's ever been," he said, checking his watch. "Which explains why she totally blew us off for lunch."

"Shopping?"

He nodded. "There's something about the word boutique that she finds irresistible, and I know she wanted to bring a housewarming present back for Nora and Woody."

"They're moving in together?"

"Yep," he said, scooting around the table to get the sun off his back. "Maybe if you hurry up with this place, you can convince them to have a destination wedding."

"Has he proposed?"

"No, but he's been taking every shift I can give him," Ben said. "And they're getting pretty serious so I'd be surprised if it doesn't happen soon."

"Good for him."

"I know, right?" Ben reached for his lemonade. "The guy's an inspiration. He thinks I did him a favor giving him a job at the club, but to be honest, I've gotten so much out of having him around I can't even tell you."

"And what about you and Carrie?" I asked.

"What about us?"

"When are you going to walk her down the aisle?"

"I don't know," he said. "But it's not going to be here."

I smiled. "Maybe for the honeymoon?"

"Settle down, man. It's not going to happen. When the time comes, I'm going to take her to a private island or something where we can have an X-rated honeymoon without scarring other people's children."

"Fine," I said. "I take it back. You're not invited to honeymoon here."

"What about you?" he asked. "How are things going with Victoria?"

"Well I moved down here for the summer so what does that tell you?"

"That you're not quite as smitten as she is?"

I sighed. "My mom thinks the sun shines out of her ass."

Ben raised his eyebrows.

"I can assure you it doesn't. I checked."

"So why lead her on?"

"I'm not leading her on," I said. "I've been as straight up as I've ever been."

"What did you tell her about coming down here?"

"That I needed space and that work was my priority."

"Ouch," he said. "How did she take it?"

I shook my head. "Honestly? She acted like I asked her to wait for me and be my wife. She's so supportive it's annoying."

"I can see why your mom likes her."

"My mom just wants me to marry someone with money so I don't have to worry that they love me for the wrong reasons."

Ben smiled. "And you want to marry for love?"

"Don't say it with that dopey expression on your face. I'm not a fucking Disney Princess."

He laughed. "You sound like one."

"That's not it. I just don't love Victoria. She doesn't challenge me."

"She's beautiful."

"Yeah, but she's beautiful in the way crystal is beautiful."

He craned his neck forward. "What does that mean?"

"She's useless."

"She hosts a mean dinner party, though."

I rolled my eyes to the sky. "That's probably the real reason my mom likes her so much."

"Isn't that why we all like her so much?"

"She's not the one, Ben."

"So break things off."

"I tried," I said. "Several times. But she just tunes it out. I'm getting worried that she's certifiable. That's another reason I was so keen to distance myself."

"I've got bad news for you, Adam."

"What?"

"All women are crazy," he said. "It's just a matter of whose brand of crazy is something you can live with."

"I don't have the energy for Victoria's brand." I took a sip of water. "She's nice, but nice isn't enough. And she's pretty, but she's fake as fuck."

"Are we talking about her tits or her personality now?"

"You noticed?" I asked.

"Sorry- which one are we talking about?"

"Both."

"Then yes."

I ran a hand through my hair. "I figured as much. Unfortunately, my relationship with Victoria seems to be one of the few things that brings my mom comfort these days."

"That's tough, man."

"Yeah." I watched a dragonfly hover over a nearby table. "But that doesn't change the fact that I want to meet someone real, someone hot who makes me laugh and isn't a suck up."

Ben tilted his glass against his mouth and crunched some ice cubes.

"You know what I mean?"

"I do," he said. "But have you ever met someone you would describe that way?"

"Once," I said. "A long time ago."

THREE
- Jolie -

"I think it's pretty obvious why she didn't ask for your opinion," Gia said from behind the reception desk as she rolled up the sleeves of her white shirt.

I rested an elbow on the counter between us. "What do you mean?"

She shrugged as she scanned the lobby. "I mean she knew you wouldn't be cool with it."

"Of course I'm not cool with it," I said, struggling to not raise my voice. "My dad built this place with his bare hands and then put every penny he ever made back into it. It was supposed to stay in the family."

"She obviously had no choice."

I shook my head. "I don't buy it. Everyone always has a choice."

Gia cocked her head. "I don't mean to be disagreeable, Jo, but I don't think your mom would've made this decision if her back wasn't up against the wall."

I squinted at her. "How can you take her side right now?"

"I'm not taking her side," Gia said, pushing her long black braid behind her back. "All I'm saying is that there's only one person that was more adversely affected by your dad's death than you."

I sighed. "I know." Of course I knew. My mom's collapse into despair had been the elephant in the room for the last two years.

And it was confusing because part of me felt some sick satisfaction at how visibly broken up she was, as if I were relieved to discover that she felt as lost without him as I did. Still, I couldn't help but wish she'd suck it up and be stronger- not only for me, but for herself, too.

It would've broken his heart to see her dragging her feet around and recoiling from all the things they used to like doing together.

I couldn't remember the last time she went golfing, and I'd offered to go to the movies with her, but it was like everything that was even remotely relaxing or entertaining filled her with so much guilt and sadness over my dad that she would rather give up than go on.

And while I was resenting it more with each passing day, I never thought she would do something as rash as sell his baby.

"You know what the worst part is?" I asked.

"Besides the fact that some fat, moley businessman is about to come in here, fire half the staff, wipe away all the resort's personality, and sell the place again?"

My eyes grew wide. "Okay, that sucks."

"I know," she said. "That's why I said besides that. What were you going to say?"

"She asked me to pretend to be happy with it."

Her eyes drooped at the corners.

"She broke my heart and then asked me to be strong for the staff and help them see what a good thing it was."

She shook her head. "I don't know how you're supposed to do that when you don't like anything about the situation."

"I know." I ran a hand through my hair and smiled at some customers as they walked out the front door. "Can I ask you something?"

"Of course."

"Do you think I'm being an ungrateful brat?"

"No."

"Really?" I asked. "Because you're the only person I actually trust to tell me if I'm being an idiot."

"Really, Jo."

I bit the inside of my cheek.

"You've been running this place for the last two years," she said. "The fact that your mom made this decision without consulting you is as insulting as it is a reflection on her reduced mental capacity. And you know I love your mom so I wouldn't say that lightly."

I nodded.

"But she's right," Gia said. "Everyone is going to look to you on this. It's only natural. So it might be in your best interest to feign a relaxed attitude to the new boss so your dissent doesn't trickle down to the guest's experience."

"True," I said. "Disgusting, but true."

My eyes scanned the light filled lobby. Sure, the carpet was worn and the furniture in the entry way could've been more modern, but our guests were always smiling and wasn't that the most important thing?

Yes, some of our TripAdvisor reviews had begun to mention the fact that the place needed some TLC, but no one ever had a bad word to say about the staff or their holiday or the food. Why couldn't my mom see how much potential the place still had? Why couldn't she fight as hard as my dad had for it- every day until his last?

"I know what would cheer you up," Gia said, her dark red lips curling into a smile.

"A sedative?"

"I said, up, Jolie. Not down."

"You want to go paddle boarding later?"

She scrunched her face. "Actually, I had a land based activity in mind."

I raised my eyebrows.

"Let's go out with Brian and Carlos tonight and drink till it feels like yesterday when none of this shit was even looking at the fan."

"Brian doesn't really do it for me."

She tilted an ear towards me. "He did it for you last weekend."

"Only because my blood alcohol level was so high my defenses were down."

"Seemed like you were having a pretty good time to me."

"You're right," I said. "I'm being unfair. I did have a good time, and he's a perfectly nice guy."

"With a fantastic body and a helluva lot in common with you."

"Like what?" I asked. "The fact that he likes paddle boarding and is a lousy dancer?"

"As long as he's not lousy in bed."

I looked around to make sure no one was within earshot. "He wasn't exactly lousy, but if I'd been wearing socks, he wouldn't have knocked them off or anything."

"Look," she said. "I don't want to be too harsh because it feels like enough of a victory that you actually gave him a chance, but you have to stop comparing everyone to Mr. Summer Fling from all those years ago."

I sighed. "I know. He totally ruined me. He actually made me believe it was possible to have sex with someone you didn't know that well and not regret it the next day."

"I think you're too harsh a critic."

"And I think I'm one of those women who's cursed by the fact that the best sex of my life is behind me."

She raised a palm at me and shook her head. "As you know, I can't relate because my first time was horrendous."

"Whereas mine turned into a summer so romantic that every guy since has seemed dull in comparison."

"Are you sure you aren't just using that guy as an excuse to not get close to anyone else?"

"Of course," I said. "I'd love to be serious about someone and have a legitimate reason to turn down creeps at the bar who want to buy me drinks."

"Mmm."

"But that guy stole my ignorance when he took my innocence, and now I can't just settle for someone who's nice or merely… inoffensive."

Gia cocked her head. "How lucky for me that I'm not burdened by such high standards."

"I didn't mean it like that."

She smiled. "I know, but the fact of the matter is that he was just a summer crush and he disappeared a lifetime ago. It's not like he's going to suddenly be… on the other side of the room."

"I understand that, but-"

"No. Jolie."

I furrowed my brow. "What?"

"I'm serious."

I stared into her big brown eyes. They were looking right past me.

"Isn't that him?" she asked.

I rolled my eyes. "Don't fuck with me, Gia. That's not cool."

"I'm not," she said, her voice dropping to a whisper. "That guy looks just like him."

"Where?" I asked, looking over my shoulder.

"By the stand that holds the pamphlets for all the local tours."

My eyes darted towards the front door.

And sure enough, there he was.

The only boy I ever loved.

Except there was nothing boyish about him anymore.

And while my first thought was that my mind was playing tricks on me, as far as my body was concerned, there was absolutely no question.

It was him.

And he was taller, better dressed, and more handsome than ever.

FLASHBACK
- Jolie -

I'd just gotten in trouble for talking back to my mom.

Gia and I were playing in the pool, and we took a noodle from some other kid to secure the foundation on our spectacular noodle fort.

Unfortunately, the victim of our thievery was a paying guest at the hotel. So when my mom realized what we'd done, Gia got sent to join her mom on housekeeping duty, and I was sent to the edge of the pool deck with a worn out toothbrush and some grout cleaner.

Worst of all, from where I was sitting in my faded Oshkosh cutoffs, I could see the victim- who'd finally stopped fake crying his butt off- living it up in our noodle fort.

I was absolutely fuming for a whole five minutes, but then something caught my eye. Just over the dunes I saw a kite, or rather, flashes of a kite.

It was blue and green and had a little trail of ribbons behind it, but it took me several flashes to get all that because it wasn't taking flight.

Instead, someone was simply throwing it in the air over and over, just high enough for it to turn around and dive straight towards the ground again.

It seemed clear to me- even at such a young age- that the person either didn't know how to fly a kite or was lacking in the assistance they needed to help the thing take off.

Being an independent minded sort of kid, it occurred to me that assisting another guest might be equally fair penance for my selfish noodle thieving.

Obviously, I didn't bother asking my mom if she agreed. After all, she was already annoyed with me, and it was very likely she would say no, especially since she knew how much I loved kites and hated scrubbing grout.

So, like a martyr, I walked down the path over the dunes, my curious brown eyes trained on the jumping kite I'd never seen before.

When the kite's owner came into view, I could tell by the twisted expression on his sun kissed face that he was getting frustrated.

"Hi," I said, guessing he was around my age once I'd walked up to get a closer look.

"Hi," he said. "Can you give me some space?" He threw the kite in the air again.

"Are you fishing for birds?" I asked.

The kite crashed down in the sand between us.

He exhaled and looked at me. "You're not very funny."

"And you're not very good at flying kites."

"I almost had it that time."

"No you didn't," I said. "But don't worry. I can help. My name's Jolie, and I work here."

He furrowed his brow and picked up the kite. "You work where?"

I pointed a thumb behind me. "At the Harmony Bay Hotel."

He glanced over my shoulder. "Aren't you a little young to have a job?"

"No," I said. "I have a lot of jobs."

He squinted at me.

"And one of them is helping people fly kites."

"I don't need help," he said, taking a step back.

I scrunched my face. I wasn't used to people being so difficult. "Then I have bad news."

He raised his eyebrows.

"I can't allow you to keep flying your kite if you don't accept help."

He craned his neck back. "What?"

I put my hands on my hips. "The people on the pool deck are getting very depressed about your kite."

"Depressed?"

I nodded. "It's ruining their view of the beach."

He looked back and forth between me and the kite.

"But if you can get it airborne, then we won't have any problems."

"Sorry," he said. "I didn't know that was a rule."

"It's okay. Now you know."

He pressed his lips together and looked at the reel in his hand.

I widened my stance like my dad always did when he was giving instructions. "You have to unravel a lot more string than that if you want to give the kite a flying chance."

The boy handed the kite to me and started unraveling the string.

"More," I said when he raised his eyes. "Keep going. I'll say when… Okay, that's enough."

"Now what?"

I looked over my shoulder at the sea oats on the dunes to figure out which way the wind was blowing. "Now run that way as fast as you can," I said, pointing down the beach.

"What are you going to do?"

"I'm going to release the kite into the air at the perfect moment."

He pushed his thick brown hair out of his eyes.

"Trust me," I said. "This isn't my first rodeo."

"Rodeo?"

I groaned. "It's an expression. Doesn't your mom ever watch Dr. Phil?"

He shook his head.

"Just run already."

He wiggled his toes in the sand and took off a second later.

"Faster!" I called as I watched the string at my feet disappear. "And don't look back!" I yelled when he glanced over his shoulder.

Finally, I counted to three, jumped as high as I could, and threw the kite straight into the air.

And like magic, it took off.

When the string went taut, he turned but kept running backwards, a huge smile spreading across his face. "Thanks!" he shouted.

The wind brought his gratitude drifting past my ears.

When he tripped on some driftwood a moment later, I saw the panic in his face that the kite might fall, too, but he held fast to the reel and stood up, dusting off his sandy bottom as I jogged down the beach to make sure he could take it from there.

And from that moment on, our friendship- like the kite- had wings.

FOUR
- Adam -

I was used to being the boss, but I'd never attempted what I could only assume would be interpreted as a hostile takeover before.

I didn't want to be the bad guy, but to some extent, I knew there would be little I could do to avoid that. And while I wasn't normally one to rule with an iron fist, making the right first impression would be imperative if I was going to get these people to trust me and follow my lead.

After all, my dad was a venture capitalist, and I'd seen him flip enough companies to know that there was no point in trying to be everyone's best friend when there was money at stake.

My only option was to come in strong without giving off a whiff of weakness. Then, once my authority was established and I'd earned everyone's respect, I could loosen the reigns and start handing out smiles and attaboys.

Of course, there was one person I was prepared to make an exception for, and as the staff gathered in the conference room, I watched from a corner table, sipped my coffee, and waited for her arrival.

When she walked in, I felt my whole body tighten.

She was as striking as I remembered. Her long, sun kissed brown hair swung behind her as she walked in, her tan legs sticking out of her figure hugging skirt. It was too long for my liking as the memory of her legs flashed through my mind, but she looked good in her professional attire. Unwrappable.

She was another reason I'd bought the place.

Because while I'd tried to convince myself otherwise, I knew deep down that the summer I finally had her was the best summer of my life.

Sure, I was well aware that buying a failing hotel was an extreme action to take just to satisfy my curiosity about a young woman I'd been unable to forget, but if I was going to come down and see what she was like all these years later, I didn't see why I shouldn't mix business with pleasure.

That way, at least if I didn't get the girl, I'd have some money to show for my efforts.

Not that I was about to admit any of that out loud.

I couldn't. The whole idea was ridiculous.

What self-respecting man falls in love with the first girl he sleeps with?

She didn't know she was my first, of course. I didn't dare tell her. I liked the way she looked at me, as if she trusted that I was more experienced than she was. I got the sense she wanted me to be, and I wanted to be exactly what she wanted.

When we bumped into each other as kids, I always considered her a jovial playmate, but that last summer everything changed. It had been a few years since I'd seen her and in that time, we'd both grown up and changed shape.

And I knew when I gave her that first kiss that one would never be enough.

She was also the second woman I ever slept with. And the third, fourth, fifth, and who knew how many times after that. There were too many romps to count, though I remembered each stolen moment vividly.

I liked her because she was different than anyone I knew back home, and when you mix an exotic, beautiful girl with a summer of carnal pleasures, what young man isn't going to become intoxicated?

Back then I assumed she would eventually be nothing more than a fond memory. I assumed the sound of her laugh and the image of her face would blur around the edges and then in the middle, like all my other memories seemed to do in the end.

But that hadn't happened.

My sense of her stayed sharp, and my longing for her never went away.

She made me understand what that expression "to get under someone's skin" meant, for she was very much under mine.

After some quick research, it was easy enough to confirm that her parents still owned the place, and after speaking with her mother, it was obvious that she'd become overwhelmed with the task of running it. She volunteered that Jolie had pretty much taken over.

I felt sick when I heard her dad had passed away. I remembered his face from when we were young and he used to call her in from the beach while we were in the middle of digging a hole or collecting sand crabs.

I had this awful feeling over the fact that she'd had to go through his death without me, that I hadn't been there to lend my support.

Which was absurd.

I didn't even know her that well.

That's when I realized I wished I did. And I knew if I didn't come down to Harmony Bay immediately, I might miss my chance to know her better.

Or know her again… at least once or twice.

Because a girl like Jolie wasn't going to be single forever, and her mom had let it slip that she currently was when she'd mentioned that she'd become a bit of a workaholic.

All through college, I dated women from my own social circles, women from big cities or upstate, women who were perfectly lovely and educated.

I'd hoped one of them might get under my skin.

But it never happened.

And sleeping with them had never matched the thrill I got from being with Jolie that summer. On the beach. In her car. In the woods by the 18th hole.

She was the only girl I wanted to see more of, the only girl I ever regretted not calling.

Still, coming down here had been a leap of faith.

Not only was I taking a chance on the hotel, but I was gambling big on the fact that she would remember me.

And if she did, would she even be happy to see me?

Only time would tell.

I waited a few minutes past the scheduled meeting time to accommodate a few late arrivals before clearing my throat and walking up to the front of the room.

"Hello everyone," I said. "Thanks for coming on such short notice. I know you run a tight ship here so I won't take much of your time."

The quiet murmurs of the staff stopped and people grew still in their seats while those standing around the perimeter of the room- Jolie included- stopped rocking on their heels.

"My name is Adam Darling, and I am the proud new owner of the Harmony Bay Resort Hotel." I stood with my feet shoulder width apart and moved my hands deliberately while I spoke. "I'm delighted to say I recognize a lot of you as my family spent many summer vacations here when I was growing up. In fact, some of my fondest memories were made on the grounds of this hotel." It took everything I had not to look at her. "So it's a place that's very dear to my heart."

Everyone's eyes were on me.

"I know it was also very dear to Mr. Monroe- may he rest in peace- and after my conversations with his wife, I feel well versed on what his original mission was for this place, what his values were, and how highly he regarded each and every one of you. Yes, I plan to make some big changes around here, but rest assured, it is his original dream for this place that will inform every decision I make."

I took a deep breath. "That being said, I look forward to getting to know each of you while making it a great summer for the hotel and our guests."

FIVE
- Jolie -

How dare he come in here and act like he knew what my father stood for.

So what if he liked the beach and our chicken fingers and our complimentary boogie boards, he didn't know what we were about and he sure as hell wasn't part of our family.

And he didn't even look at me once! What an unbelievable prick?!

My dad always said people with too much money were inhumane, and it seemed Adam's upbringing had finally spoilt him like the rest. And the fact that my mom would sell the place to a soulless rich guy sickened me at her decision all over again.

Worst of all, the fact that I was still attracted to him felt like an extreme betrayal. I felt ashamed that I hadn't worked harder to forget him, to get over him, to forget the ridiculous hyperbolic compliments I'd paid him as we laid in the back of the golf cart and under the stars and behind the pool house.

Ugh.

How could I have been so stupid? He wasn't god's gift to me. He was more like the devil incarnate, and now I had to pretend to like him when all I really liked was his square jaw and dark eyes and the way he looked in his cobalt suit. Damn it.

When he was finally done speaking, I stepped back and lingered at the edge of the room, trying to gauge the morale of the staff as they returned to their regular duties.

Some of them seemed relieved, as if they were looking forward to having him onboard. As if they actually believed a word that came out of his mouth.

Meanwhile, others seemed skeptical, as if they inherently sensed that there was nothing he wouldn't have said to get us onside. After all, how else could he get us to lower our guard so he could bulldoze over us with the vision he had for the place?

"Is it possible that he doesn't remember you?" Gia asked under her breath as she folded her arms.

I forced a smile at the staff trickling by. "It feels that way, doesn't it?"

"He didn't even look over here once," she said. "That's pretty cold."

"Yeah."

"I know it was just a summer fling, but-"

"Not a word of that to anyone," I said, raising a finger at her. "Promise me."

She lifted her palms between us. "I promise. Obviously. I'm just saying I'm surprised."

"Me too."

"Maybe he just didn't see you."

I cocked my head at her.

She shrugged. "You have a better explanation?"

"No. But he's going to fucking see me alright." I turned my eyes back to the far end of the room where he was talking to an attractive blonde I'd never seen before.

"What are you going to do?" she asked.

"I'm going to tell him that he might have bought this place, but he doesn't own it."

"I don't think breaking the ice with blatant inaccuracies is going to earn his respect or attention."

"I don't want his attention," I lied, recalling the first time he caused a spark to shoot up my spine. He'd wrapped his fingers around the base of my neck and pressed his thumb against my racing pulse. No one had ever touched me like that. No one had ever looked me in the eyes as they felt my heart beating. It made me feel possessed and attractive and aroused and a bunch of other things I didn't even have the words for then.

"What do you want then?" Gia asked.

"I want him to go away and never come back."

She laughed.

I shot her a look. "What's so funny?"

She smiled. "You're too much."

I craned my neck back. "Excuse me?"

"You spend every spare second for the last six years doodling this guy's name in the sand and thinking about him while you touch yourself at night-"

"Remind me to never confide in you again."

She dropped her chin. "And then he shows up and you want to ring his neck."

"I'm just as surprised as you are."

"If I had to guess," she said, "I'd say your hots for him haven't cooled a bit, and you're only digging your heels in because he's the new boss."

"Wrong."

"Really?" she asked. "Because I think if he showed up at Castaways and tried to buy you a drink, you'd slide off your fricking bar stool."

"I would not."

"You so would," she said. "And I bet he'd catch you, too, because he seems like the kind of guy whose hands are never too full."

"I don't know what that means."

"It means he's hot."

"Gia!"

"What? I'm not saying I'm happy to see him or anything. I'm just stating the obvious."

I winced.

"Surely you can at least admit that he's even better looking than he was when he was seventeen."

I glared across the room. "His shoulders might be a little broader, but that's it."

"If I remember your eye witness accounts correctly, it wasn't just the breadth of his shoulders that impressed you."

"Stop it," I said, raising my eyebrows. "You're not helping."

"Fine," she said, her mouth curling into a smile. "So you don't see it. No biggie."

"Thanks."

"Does that mean you're cool with me making a pass because he makes Carlos look like a White Castle Slider."

I narrowed my eyes at her.

"Whereas he's a filet mignon."

I groaned. "First of all, no to your analogy. Second of all, no to you sleeping with the boss. And finally, no to you even making a pass. It's not appropriate."

"That's what I thought," she said, smirking. "Once your dream guy, always your dream guy."

I sighed. "Please don't torment me. I'm under enough pressure to act like this isn't the worst day of my life."

"Fine. I'll back off," she said. "But I can't say the same for her."

I looked back towards Adam and watched as the pretty blonde girl held his attention, laying out what appeared to be swatches of fabric that didn't match a single room in the hotel.

"He's going to change everything," I whispered.

"Except your mind apparently."

I turned back around. "What do you mean?"

"I mean you're not going to sleep with him no matter what? Not for old time's sake? Or to confirm whether or not he's as good as you remembered him to be?"

"Of course not."

She nodded. "Okay. Just checking."

"Do you really think I would sink that low?"

She pressed her lips together.

My mouth fell open.

"All I know is that twenty four hours ago, you would've cried happy tears if you thought that guy was coming to town."

I crossed my arms. "That was yesterday."

"Then maybe you were right," she said, turning towards the door.

"About what?" I asked, furrowing my brow.

"About the fact that your love life is obviously cursed."

SIX
- Adam -

"That wasn't exactly the warm reception I was hoping for," I said, heading for the nearest chair.

"Don't worry about it," Carrie said, laying fabric swatches on the table beside me like she was putting together a puzzle. "It's not your fault. The previous owner clearly didn't give anyone a heads up that she was going to sell the place."

"Maybe that's why I feel so unsettled. Everyone just looked shocked."

"It will take some time getting them to warm to you, but that's true of any takeover situation. Once we fix up the first room and they see that you've actually come to help as opposed to suck them dry-"

"Suck who dry?"

I looked up towards the familiar voice. Jolie was standing on the opposite side of the table with her arms crossed and her hip cocked.

Carrie's warm smile failed to melt Jolie's icy expression. "I was just saying that once you all see the nice improvements we make aesthetically, you'll realize that Adam means you no harm."

I stood up. "Carrie, this is Mrs. Monroe's daughter. She's the general manager."

"Oh." Carrie walked around the table and extended a hand. "I'm Carrie. Adam brought me down to help update the hotel's décor."

Jolie took her hand reluctantly. "Jolie," she said. "And I'm not sure what Adam's told you, but this is my hotel, and I'm the one that needs to okay any changes you plan to make. Not him."

Carrie raised her eyebrows at me and forced a smile. "Of course."

I nodded. "Jolie's right. She knows this place inside out and the customers better than anyone- some more than others," I said, fixing my eyes on her until she blushed.

"So when it comes time to choose flower arrangements and curtains, please consider her the boss."

"I do a lot more than pick the flowers around here," Jolie snapped. "Which you'd know if you hadn't just barged in like you own the place."

I raised my eyebrows. "I do own the place."

Carrie's eyes bounced back and forth between us. "I can see that you two have some catching up to do," she said, opening her purse and sweeping the piled swatches into it. "I'll go find Ben and catch up with you later, Adam. Nice to meet you, Jolie." She nodded as she took off, looking back at me with wide eyes after she'd passed Jolie.

"Who's Ben?" Jolie asked. "Someone else that doesn't know the place and feels compelled to stick his nose where it doesn't belong?"

I rested my fingers on the table. "Actually, Ben's a friend of mine."

She scoffed.

"He's in the hospitality business himself, and his father owns the most successful luxury hotel chain in the world."

She swallowed.

"I thought he might come in handy."

She looked over her shoulder at the empty conference room behind her.

I used the moment to scan her from head to toe, letting myself wonder if her body was as sensitive as it once was, as tight all over- yet soft in all the right places.

Unfortunately, by the time I was done checking her out, her eyes were back on me, and the face she was making suggested I'd been caught in the act.

"What are you doing here, Adam?" she asked, resting her shiny nails on the opposite side of the table.

"Have a seat," I said, pulling out a chair.

"I'd rather stand."

I squinted. "You seem angrier than I remember."

She straightened up. "You remember me?"

"Of course I remember you," I said, sitting down. "I remember everything."

She pressed her glossy lips together.

"I remember how you smell," I said, leaning back. "How you taste."

Her light brown eyes grew wide.

"I remember the sound of your laugh, and the noise you used to make when I slid my hand in your bikini bottoms-"

"That's enough."

"It never was for me," I said, crossing an ankle over my knee. "And I don't recall you ever tiring of it."

"Look," she said, lowering her voice. "I'm flattered that you remember me, but that's all in the past and things are different now."

I cocked my head. "Are they? Because I'm pretty sure I'm still the boss and you still want me to tell you what to do."

"That is so not what I want," she said. "And if you think this-" She pointed back and forth between us. "Is going to happen, then you're an even bigger idiot than I thought."

"What's with the hostility, Jo?"

"Don't call me that."

"I thought we had something special?"

"We did." She tucked a strand of hair behind her triple pierced ear. "But that was before you showed up and took what wasn't yours."

"That's not at all how I see it."

She raised her eyebrows. "How do you see it?"

I rolled my eyes up to the ceiling. "I see it more like I take what I want and I make it mine."

"Like my dad's hotel?"

"Among other things."

"Why are you doing this?" she asked.

"Because your mom made me an offer I couldn't refuse."

She clenched her jaw.

"Besides, I wanted to see you."

"If you wanted to see me, you knew where I was."

"I know," I said. "That made it very easy to find you."

"You didn't have to buy the place."

"No," I said. "But why does anyone do anything?"

"For fun?"

I shook my head. "No. There's only two reasons people do anything. One is love."

"Let me guess. The other's money?"

I adjusted a cufflink. "Bingo."

"I don't get what's in it for you," she said. "Why Harmony Bay?"

"Because I'm fond of this place, and I know it can be better. You know it, too, I suspect. You're just too stubborn to ask for the help your mom was wise enough to seek out."

"My mom is vulnerable right now, and you took advantage."

"Good thing it was me then instead of someone that doesn't have the hotel's best interests at heart."

She shook her head. "You think this is a joke."

"I think it's an opportunity."

"To do what?" she asked. "Destroy my family's legacy?"

"No. To save it. Among other things."

She narrowed her eyes at me. "What other things?"

"Turning it into a profitable investment for one."

"Anything else?"

"There's a woman I'd like to impress," I said. "Though it seems I'm going to have to do a lot more than save her hotel from bankruptcy to make her believe it."

She leaned forward. "You're full of shit."

"Perhaps," I said, folding my hands in my lap. "But maybe I'm fucking crazy about you and just nuts enough to do something this absurd."

"No one's that stupid."

I smiled. "Seems to me you wouldn't believe me even if I were telling the truth."

She wiped her hands on the front of her hip hugging skirt.

"Which is disappointing because it means things have changed."

"What do you mean?" she asked.

"Well, when you were seventeen, you wanted to believe everything that came out of my mouth."

"Maybe. But you were a decent guy then."

"I'm still a decent guy," I said. "You'll see."

"Don't hold your breath," she said, turning on her heels.

"One last tip before you go," I said.

She looked back over her shoulder.

"Do us both a favor and go easy on the frosty reception angle," I said, clasping my hands behind my head. "It might undermine your professionalism if it's obvious to the staff how bad you want me back."

S E V E N
- Jolie -

"At least he remembers you," Gia said, moving her chair and her margarita into the shade. "That's something, isn't it?"

"This is a disaster," I said, putting my head in my hands and sucking some mojito through my straw. "I don't know how to be professional around him any more than I know how to lead the rest of the team right now."

"Just act like you're not completely freaked out and pretend you've never shagged the guy."

I lifted my eyes towards her.

"For a start."

"Is that your best idea? Really? Just carry on like he hasn't seen me naked? Like he hasn't licked my-"

"Heard we've all got a new boss," Debbie said, replacing our complimentary bowl of spicy nuts.

"What else did you hear?" I asked, straightening up in my chair.

"I heard he's smoking hot and not wearing a ring."

"It's true," Gia said.

I shot her a look.

She shrugged.

"Bout time we had some fresh meat around here," Debbie said, surveying the surrounding patrons at the ramshackle beach bar. "If I wanted to see dad bods all day, I'd stay home with my husband."

I scrunched my face. "He's not back at work yet?"

She shook her head. "Nope. Worst of all, I'm starting to think he's happy sitting on his ass all day watching day time television and letting me bring home the bacon."

I made a mental note to tip her generously when we left. "Sorry, Deb. That must be hard on you."

"I don't mean to complain," she said. "He's a good man, and I'm better off with his love in my life."

"I'm sure he'll go back to work as soon as his back's a hundred percent," Gia said. "He's probably just being cautious so he doesn't get hurt again."

"Can I get you girls anything else?" she asked, eyeing our glasses.

"I think we're okay for the minute," I said. "But we won't be shy if we need something."

Debbie nodded and moved on to a table down the beach covered in empty beer bottles.

"So you up for a night out with the guys?" Gia asked. "To take your mind off Mr. Too Hot to Handle?"

I furrowed my brow. "Can we not give him stupid nicknames?"

"I was going to go with Mr. Untouchable, but something tells me he's very touchable indeed."

I cocked my head. "Carlos wouldn't appreciate you talking about another guy like that."

"Yeah, well, I don't appreciate the fact that he thinks his best chance of finding a decent job is playing video games until he 'gets noticed' and one of the gaming companies invites him to play professionally."

"Is that even a thing?"

"Apparently," she said. "I guess they employee people to play the games all day and look for glitches."

"Wouldn't that take all the fun out of it for him?"

She craned her neck forward. "Is that really what disturbs you most about the situation?"

"I thought he was tutoring Spanish this summer?"

"He is," she said. "When it doesn't interfere with his gaming."

I shook my head. "We have to stop messing with boys."

"At least Brian has a regular nine to five."

"I feel like we need to set our standards higher than just employed."

"Probably," she said. "But we know all the locals and everyone else is only here for the summer."

"It does feel like a hamster wheel."

"No shit," she said. "Neither of us has ever dated a guy that couldn't be described as a summer boyfriend. Doesn't that seem odd to you?"

"Maybe updating the hotel will bring a younger crowd through," I said. "That would actually be an improvement I could get excited about."

"At the very least it would improve our spring break prospects."

"And distract me from the fact that I'm insanely attracted to my new boss."

"I know," Gia said. "I'm sorry I ever convinced you to crash that party."

I sighed. "Now that you mention it, this is all your fault."

She nodded. "Maybe, but it seemed like such a good idea at the time."

"It was," I said, remembering how we crashed the beach party full of teenage guests who'd waited all day to flee their parent's supervision and drink cheap rum on the beach.

It was the first time Adam and I crossed paths that summer, and I remembered it like it was yesterday. He was standing by the bonfire, his chiseled features exaggerated in the jumping, yellow light.

I could still picture how thick his dark, windswept hair looked. He was obviously the same boy I'd once played beach games with, but he seemed more dangerous somehow. Or maybe delicious is a better word.

I swear I was in love with him after just a few swigs of rum, and when he put his heavy arm over my shoulder like I belonged to him, my insides turned to cotton candy.

Then he introduced me to his buddy as his friend, Jolie, and the fact that he remembered my name was enough to convince me that I should kiss him that night at the very least.

I never thought that night would go on to become the best month of my life.

Of course, I should've known then it would never work.

As if I could ever end up with a guy whose family could afford to go on vacation to a hotel for a whole month.

"What was his friend's name again?" I asked. "Do you remember?"

"Christophe," Gia said.

"Oh right. To be fair, that was the first time we both really liked a pair of friends equally."

Gia smiled. "He was a scoundrel."

"It's a shame that was the only summer he ever came."

Gia leaned back in her chair. "And yet he came again and again thanks to me."

"I wonder what ever happened to him."

"Betcha Adam knows," Gia said.

"I don't really think inquiring about him would lend itself to my professionalism."

Gia laughed.

"Hey Adam, whatever happened to your friend that rode the receptionist all summer? Any plans to invite him back to town?"

"You won't even consider it?" She stuck her lower lip out in a pout.

"I don't even get why you liked him. He was so rude."

"In all the best ways, though," she said, her eyes crinkling at the edges.

I lifted a palm. "Stop. I feel like I can sense your filthy thoughts from here."

"Sorry," she said, using her straw to stir the ice at the bottom of her glass. "It's been a while since I thought about him."

"Remember that night they took us out on that boat?"

She sighed. "That's when I realized I would be such a good rich guy's wife."

I rolled my eyes.

"Seriously, though. I was born to lounge around on yachts in a white bikini."

I laughed. "I think you're underselling yourself."

"No. Underselling myself is letting Carlos buy his way into my skirt for the grand total of a bucket of Coronas."

"I can't argue with that."

"It wasn't just the money," she said. "He had great hair, too."

"I know. They were really fun. I always hoped we'd run into them again on an exotic island vacation... not that we'd be forced into close proximity with just one of them in a position we didn't want him in."

"I knew you wanted to get him in another position."

"That is not what I meant," I said, raising a finger at her. "Don't twist my words."

Debbie appeared with another drink for each of us, moving them from her tray to the table carefully.

I was about to object when she offered an explanation.

"These are from the gentleman over there," she said.

I looked over my shoulder and saw Adam looking unreasonably attractive in a pair of reflective aviators with an open newspaper and a sweating beer in front of him. "Shit," I mumbled when he waved at me.

"He's taken care of your bill, too," Debbie said.

"At least let me tip you," I said, reaching for my purse on the table.

"It's all taken care of," she said, dropping her voice to a whisper. "Biggest tip I've gotten all summer."

I kept my groan on the inside.

Debbie pinned her tray against her hip. "You girls make sure you say thank you and bring him back here."

"Something tells me you don't have to worry about that," Gia said, smiling and raising her fresh glass towards him.

"What are you doing?" I asked when Debbie walked away.

"Being polite to my new boss," she said. "Obviously."

I dropped my head back for a second before staring at my free drink. "That isn't very boss like behavior."

"Maybe not," Gia said. "But you sure as shit won't hear me complaining about it."

EIGHT
- Adam -

I was delighted to discover how relaxed the atmosphere at the beach bar was. I knew it was a place my parents frequented on our trips down here, but by the time I was old enough to be interested in drinking, I was still too young to get served at the bar.

That's actually how the summer I last saw Jolie kicked off.

My buddy and I were on the beach, drinking cheap rum with a bunch of other teenagers who'd been dragged on a family holiday against their will. I still remember the way my body froze when I saw her walk up to the campfire.

Her hair was long and hung in loose waves that looked as if they'd been styled by the salty ocean breeze, and her halter top ended just above the waistband of her frayed jean shorts, allowing me an occasional glimpse of her shiny, dangling belly button ring.

She was the hottest girl I'd ever seen, and I remember being shocked that I'd been oblivious to it all those years when we were flying kites and digging holes…

I checked my watch, eager for Ben's arrival. I knew he was the man who could tell me how to turn the beach bar into a money making machine instead of a pseudo successful side hustle.

Unfortunately, it would be a while yet before he arrived so I made myself comfortable and ordered another drink.

From behind my aviators, I noticed that Gia and Jolie had finished their drinks, and after exchanging mock cheek kisses, they headed up the boardwalk towards the street.

But just as I was preparing myself for Jolie's tan legs to disappear from view, she turned towards my table and didn't stop walking until she was standing in front of me.

"If you think you can buy my loyalty and respect, you're not as smart as you look."

I lowered my newspaper and looked up at her. "That's the closest thing to a compliment you've paid me since I arrived."

"It wasn't meant to be a compliment."

"Forgive me for reading into it."

"Did you hear what I said?" she asked, cocking her hip.

"I think we've gotten off on the wrong foot," I said. "Why don't you stop embarrassing yourself and sit down for a second?"

"I don't want to si-"

"Sit down, Jolie." I hated to use such a forceful tone with her, but her hostility was starting to piss me off. "That's not an invitation. It's an order."

She pulled out the chair across from me and sat down. "Just so you know, if you ever speak to me like that again-"

"Let me guess, you only like to be bossed around when you're naked?"

Her lips fell apart.

"I think most women feel that way."

"How dare you."

"No," I said, folding my paper and leaning forward. "How dare you."

She craned her neck back. "Excuse me?"

"How dare you accuse me of trying to buy your loyalty and respect," I said, pressing a finger against the small round table. "I bought you a goddamn drink. That's it. Accept it graciously like a normal person."

She clenched her jaw.

"You think I'm amused by the chip on your shoulder?" I asked. "Do you have any idea how many chipped shoulders I have to ignore on a daily basis? Being a bitch doesn't make you unique."

She folded her arms.

"But I don't want to ignore you, okay? I want to play nice. I want things to be like they were back when we were happy to see each other."

"You mean how they were before you bought this place?"

"What does it matter?" I asked. "You haven't lost your job, and I'm here for the right reasons. I'm going to help make this resort something you can be proud of."

"I'm already proud of it."

"Yeah, I picked up on that." I leaned back in my chair. "Has it crossed your mind that maybe you should give me a chance? Has it occurred to you that this transition might be easier if you don't waste energy fighting me tooth and nail?"

She swallowed.

I raised a hand at Debbie and pointed at Jolie, who whipped around in her chair too late to cancel the drink order.

She lifted her sunglasses onto her head as she turned back around, her coconut brown eyes causing my guts to twist in a knot. "Sorry if I'm not exactly filled with confidence," she said. "But you seem to have forgotten that I've known you since you were in Spiderman trunks."

My mouth curled up on one side. "So it was my trunks you noticed first then?"

She rolled her eyes.

"Here you go," Debbie said, setting another mojito down in front of Jolie. Then she took the empty bowl between us and put some more spicy nuts down in its place.

"Thanks, Debbie," I said, nodding.

She smiled and glanced at my drink before excusing herself.

"Debbie likes you, anyway," Jolie said.

"Doesn't she have the loveliest smile?" I reached for some nuts. "Shame about her husband, though."

"You know her pretty well already, huh?"

"As far as I'm concerned, anyone with a direct line to the bar is well worth getting to know."

She scoffed.

"You disagree?"

"No," she said, crossing her legs.

"Well, now's your chance," I said, crunching another handful of nuts.

"To do what?"

"To ask me whatever's on your mind," I said. "You've obviously made some unflattering assumptions about me, and I'd like to clear the air if we're going to be working together on a daily basis."

She lifted her drink and sipped from the straw.

"You're welcome, by the way."

"I didn't ask you to get me a drink."

"That's not how manners work, actually, but let's stick a pin in that for now and get back to whatever you're so angry about."

"Where are you living this summer?" she asked. "While you're tearing apart the hotel?"

I furrowed my brow. "In the hotel, of course."

She raised her eyebrows.

"Perhaps you've forgotten, but I'm a hands on kind of guy."

She cocked her head. "In the suite, I presume?"

"Are you asking for a copy of my key?"

"No," she said. "I'm just trying to figure out how much money the hotel is going to lose out on with you living there."

"I see. Well, I figured I'd renovate the suite first and move in there when it's ready," I said. "But you can rest assured that I'll be putting several million into the hotel renovations during my stay so the hotel can afford to host me."

"Several million?"

"Give or take."

She stared at me for so long I noticed that soft reggae music had begun flowing through the speakers dotted along the edge of the tiki bar.

I took a sip of beer. "I'll have a better idea once Carrie takes the measurements she needs and draws up some plans."

"And where does someone your age get several million for a summer project?"

I squinted at her. "Why do I get the feeling that you're going to be disappointed if I say I worked my ass off for it?"

NINE
- Jolie -

"What's that supposed to mean?" I asked, resting my hand around the bottom of my cool glass.

He shrugged. "I don't know. By the way you're treating me it seems you'd rather I said I stole it from the poor like some kind of anti-Robin Hood."

"I just want to know the truth." And for him to not smell so good. Is that what people meant by musk? I mean, I had no clue what musk smelled like, but something told me it was the scent wafting across the table.

Did he smell like that everywhere? I couldn't remember what he smelled like the summer I fell so hard for him… Probably because we both reeked of rum.

But this- this was something else entirely. Something masculine, expensive. It was the kind of scent that could make a woman do very stupid things. Which is why I had to do everything in my power to maintain my cold front.

After all, if I let my guard down (especially after this fourth mojito) I was liable to start twirling my hair, batting my eyelashes, and licking my lips at him.

Then my cover would be blown, and I wouldn't have a chance in hell of him taking me seriously.

I glanced at my drink. The fragrant mint leaves were definitely not the culprit. It was him for sure, and between the intoxicating smell and his steady gaze, I was shaking inside like a shitting dog.

Ugh.

"The truth," he said, laying his paper on an empty chair. "Is that I started a business in college that really took off."

"Oh?"

"It's a company that arranges backpacking trips for college students who are short on cash and time but still determined to see the world."

Shit. That was pretty cool. I would've loved to have taken advantage of something like that... or to even have been a college student. "What's it called?"

"Backpack & Craic."

I rolled my eyes. "By craic you mean fun?"

"You've been to Ireland?"

I shook my head. "No. But my dad always wanted to go. His mother was from Donegal."

Adam nodded.

"Must be nice," I said. "Being so young and already having that kind of financial security."

"I guess, but it's not really the money that excites me. It's all the things you can do with it."

I cocked my head. "You mean you don't sit at home sniffing it while children in Indonesia sew the bills together so you can use them as toilet paper."

"I used to," he said. "But I got put off by the thought of all their dirty little hands on my toilet paper."

My eyes grew wide.

"That was a joke, Jolie. How the hell else was I supposed to respond to that ridiculous suggestion?"

"Right." Was it possible that he wasn't a completely self-centered douchebag?

"Despite what you obviously think, I haven't changed that much since you last saw me. Sure, I've been to college and managed to become my own boss, but I'm still a guy who'd rather drink rum barefoot around a campfire than anything else."

"I'm not sure that would be becoming of you anymore."

"Maybe it's you that's changed," he said.

"I haven't changed."

"Really? Because the thing I liked most about you was your gorgeous smile, and I haven't seen it a single time since I arrived."

My mouth twitched, but I stayed strong. "I'm not really interested in flirting with you if we're going to be working together."

"It's not flirting I'm interested in either," he said. "I just thought it would be gentlemanly to start there."

I shook my head. "Do you ever relax?"

"All the time." He folded his hands in his lap. "Just not around you apparently."

I glanced down at the table.

"Did you go to school?" he asked.

"No. I wanted to but when the recession hit and my dad got sick, I had to put it off."

"What did you want to go for?" he asked.

"Hospitality, obviously."

"I see. I thought there might be a chance you'd say Leisure Management."

I grabbed a small handful of nuts, deciding that nervous eating was safer than nervous drinking around this guy. "Why's that?"

"Your mom told me you're quite an accomplished paddle boarder."

I raised my eyebrows. "Did she now?"

"She did."

"What else did she say?" I asked, leaning back in my chair while trying to ignore the way the top of his shirt pulled across his broad chest.

"She said you're the reason the hotel has held on this long and that you have tons of brilliant ideas for how to bring more business and buzz to the place."

I dusted the spice of my hands. "I have a few."

"Sounds like you could've been a marketing major, too."

"I'm sure I could've done a lot of things," I said. "But I'm too busy to sit around wishing over my couldas and shouldas."

"For what it's worth, you can learn more about marketing and hospitality working at a place like this than you can in a classroom full of case studies."

"That's what I try to tell myself anyway."

"It's true," he said. "And I really want to hear all your ideas. I know you're the expert on how things work around here."

I licked my salty lips. "I'm glad that's obvious to you."

"It is. And I hope you believe me when I say that I intend to make your life easier over the next few months, not harder."

"Time will tell," I said, lifting my glass and using my straw to crush the mint leaves against the bottom.

He took a sip of his beer, his eyes on me the whole time, and as his Adam's apple bobbed in his throat, I felt my insides clench.

"How come you never came back?"

"After that summer?" he asked, his eyes searching mine so thoroughly I felt like he could see the memories of us I cherished most.

I nodded.

"My mom got sick and couldn't travel for a while," he said. "We couldn't take her away from her doctors."

I furrowed my brow. "Is she okay now?"

"Depends on who you ask."

"I'm asking you."

"To make a long story short, she's riddled with cancer. So no, she's not okay. At the same time, the specialists never thought she'd live this long so by some stroke of grace, she's managed to defy some pretty shitty odds."

"I'm sorry," I said. "And happy for her at the same time, I guess."

"Me too."

"How's her quality of life?"

"Not great," he said. "My dad thinks she's just holding on until she sees me married off."

"Wow. No pressure."

He laughed. "Pressure is something I'm comfortable with. It's the not knowing whether he's right that keeps me awake at night."

I narrowed my eyes at him.

"Makes me wonder if I should hurry up and do my part to put her out of her misery or never settle down in the hopes that she'll keep fighting."

"Can I be honest with you?" I asked.

"Please."

"I don't think it's healthy for you to put that on yourself."

He sighed. "I know, but sometimes the world asks us to bear burdens we didn't ask for. That's just life."

"I know what you mean."

"Yeah," he said, the corners of his eyes forming gentle creases. "I suppose you do."

TEN
- Adam -

I spent all morning clearing up the office so I could actually think in there.

After all, I had to have a headquarters of sorts, and while I'd been tempted to use my hotel room in the off chance Jolie stopped by with her guard down, I didn't really want the rest of the staff in my personal space.

Unfortunately, there wasn't much progress I could make until I figured out what was actually important.

So in the meantime, I figured the least I could do was get all the filing boxes together in one corner of the office until I could get someone in who was qualified to make sense of what I suspected would be some discouraging numbers.

And while clearing a few desk drawers was only a small gesture, it did wonders for my piece of mind.

By the time I was burned out from my blitz clean, I swear just opening that top drawer and seeing nothing but a note pad and a new pen gave me the same charge that other people got from an hour of meditation.

It's not that I couldn't handle chaos. I just felt it was important for everyone to have a small corner of the world that was tidy and had its shit together. It was my version of a lucky charm: The nearly empty drawer. I could sigh just calling it to mind.

Then again, the lucky drawer did little to mitigate the frustration I'd felt ever since I saw Jolie on my morning jog. I was nearly back at the hotel- my feet stomping along the damp sand so I wouldn't fuck up my calves in the softer stuff- when I saw her on the horizon.

I wasn't sure it was her at first, but as I squinted through my own sweat, I was able to block out enough sun to see her.

She was paddle boarding by herself out on the water, her shoulders swiveling as she moved gracefully on the surface like a mirage.

And there was something captivating about how solitary and strong she looked as her slim silhouette moved in slow motion in front of the sunrise.

As crazy as it sounds, it gave me the same feeling I always had when I saw a healthy horse in the middle of a field. It was as if her beauty and strength were so immense that I was forced to question if she was actually of this Earth.

I knew it was a ridiculous thought to have, and yet I couldn't stop myself from having it on loop as I cooled down, got a shower, and went about reorganizing the office.

Not that being preoccupied with her was anything new.

After our drink yesterday, I felt I'd made progress. She'd softened for fleeting moments here and there, and it had given me hope that she might eventually warm to me, which would be a relief since I was way past being warm for her.

It was funny though. When I arrived, I was curious if our juvenile puppy love would be reignited, but the sensation of seeing her again was more like I'd scratched the shit out of a dormant mosquito bite until it flared up again.

In other words, my attraction to her seemed as useless and it was distracting.

Fortunately, I had plenty to worry about besides her hourglass figure and whether or not she still had a belly button ring I might be able to take between my teeth.

If I didn't get this hotel back into the black, I was going to screw up what had begun as a genuinely noble exploit.

Sure, I could've simply donated a lump sum to charity like all the Tom, Dick, and Christophes I grew up with, but I always felt that giving one's time was a far more generous and powerful investment.

Granted, I had fairly deluded personal reasons for choosing Harmony Bay as my first location to put this idea into practice, but if I pulled it off, the impact the resort's newfound success could have on the community would be a gift that kept on giving for generations.

Plus, it wasn't the only project I looked at.

I'd carefully considered devoting my time to the school for girls my mom had founded in South Africa, and there was an orphanage in New Orleans my dad helped rebuild after Katrina that always needed something.

However, I wanted to make some money out of my charitable sweat. What's more, I wanted to enjoy my summer, and I had a soft spot for Harmony Bay.

How could I not? It was the only place I ever got to be a kid growing up.

Between my being an only child and the music lessons, sports practice, and academic tutors my mom had me shuttled between every day, I never had time to eat dirt and throw sand or learn to share and initiate my own friendships.

Those were all things I only got to do here when my helicopter parents let me loose with other kids and actually got tipsy enough to allow me some much needed freedom.

It's not that I was ungrateful for my privileged and highly scheduled childhood, but I wouldn't have used the word fun to describe it.

Perhaps that's why Jolie became such an important character in my life. It was like she was from another world.

She was responsible as a result of being so tied to the hotel's daily activities, but she also had a sense of adventure and a lack of fear that I'd never known in someone my age. She wasn't afraid to get stuck in, and she certainly never worried about getting dirty, wet, or sweaty.

Meanwhile, the girls I grew up with were always hell bent on keeping their little hands and dresses pristine, as if they believed- even as children- that their appearance mattered more than what they were physically and mentally capable of.

But with Jolie, it was like I could have boyish fun with someone who was much easier on the eye. And she was no girlier now- apart from her looks. But I suppose she couldn't help them.

Whatever.

I'd worked with gorgeous women before. If anything, I should've been sighing with relief over the fact that she wasn't prepared to fall at my feet like the rest of them because I was sick of that sycophantic crap.

Still, her obvious ability to resist my charms was frustrating.

And the more she refused to admit that what we had all those years ago wasn't just a bunch of misdirected hormones colliding, the more obsessed I was going to become over proving it to her.

Because I was used to getting what I wanted, and I'd never wanted anything more than I wanted to get to the bottom of my obsession with Jolie Monroe, the only girl I couldn't forget.

The only girl I'd ever lost sleep over.

E L E V E N
- Jolie -

It was too early to tell how the staff were coping.

A handful of lifers made a point of telling me they thought it would be great for fresh eyes to breathe new life into the place, but it was hard to tell if they were just being supportive because they were concerned about their jobs or whether they genuinely felt that way.

And of course the kids we only brought in for the summer couldn't have cared less about the long term state of the resort. They just wanted their seven fifty an hour with no trouble.

"Any idea what the meeting's about?" Gia asked.

"No," I said, trying not to give away how much that very fact irked me.

"Maybe we're all getting fat bonuses?"

I shot her a look. "I assure you that's not it."

"Hey, a girl can dream."

"And dream on," I said, slowing my pace as we joined the crowd funneling into the main banquet hall.

"All I'm saying is that I wouldn't be surprised if it was a morale boosting announcement."

"Why the optimism?" I asked.

"I looked into his other company."

I raised my eyebrows.

"Just online," she said. "It's got the highest ratings on Glassdoor I've ever seen."

"Really?"

She nodded. "There wasn't a single nasty post about the guy."

"Interesting."

"So he might not be as bad as you think."

I scoffed. "Or he's powerful enough to rig any system he wants, and those ratings aren't even genuine."

"I prefer to hope they are," she said.

We settled in a space between some tall white curtains and waited for the last few staff members to trickle in.

"Okay," Adam said, clearing his throat at the front of the room. He was dressed immaculately in a crisp white shirt and pants that hugged him in all the right places. He certainly looked the part of the boss, anyway.

I had to give him that. At least he hadn't shown up and mocked us in an open Hawaiian shirt and cargo shorts on day one.

"So," he said, rubbing his hands together. "Thanks for being on time. I admit I hate meetings as much as you probably do so I'll make it brief so you can get back to work."

"I don't believe for a second the guy hates meetings," Gia said. "He obviously loves the sound of his own voice."

To be honest, so did I. I mean, I didn't give a shit what he was about to say or anything, but his low tone and slight Northeastern accent was pretty seductive.

First Love

Unfortunately, something told me he wasn't about to read out the winning lotto numbers.

"In the last week, I've had a chance to get to know you all a bit on paper, but I know that most resumes aren't worth the paper they're printed on."

A few too many people laughed.

"So here's the deal. I'd like to schedule a time to meet with each of you for a few minutes so I can formally introduce myself and figure out if you prefer to go by Kathleen or Kathy- that kind of thing. Because I know this place is a family and right now I feel a bit like the estranged Uncle that nobody knows, which is a situation I'm eager to correct."

I groaned on the inside.

"Though I do want to thank those of you who've gone out of your way to welcome me, especially Jolie Monroe." He fixed his eyes on me. "Who's been very accommodating and is even more eager than I am to get this place updated, advertised, and booked solid for the next five summers."

"Oh shit," Gia whispered. "No he didn't."

"I'm going to kill him," I said, smiling through gritted teeth.

"That was pretty smooth," she said. "Everyone bought it like Black Friday."

"He's an idiot," I said, locking my eyes on him.

"Anyway." He moved his large hands through the air as he continued. "I've put a spreadsheet up in the staff kitchen so you can all choose a suitable time slot."

My stomach flipped when I realized how easy it would be for a guy like him to charm the staff one by one.

"But before you come see me-"

Everyone's eyebrows rose with mine.

"I want each of you to go online- somewhere like Monster.com- and I want you to find three jobs that you'd love to have." He squared his shoulders towards the front row. "They don't even have to be jobs you're qualified for. Just pick three that, if they were offered to you tomorrow, you'd walk straight out of here and never look back."

A soft murmur bubbled up from the group.

"What the heck?" Gia asked. "That's the craziest bull I ever heard."

My heart sank. Was he getting ready to lay people off or just trying to alienate them? I swear I felt like I could feel the seeds of discontent he'd just thrown over the group sprouting between the legs of the chairs they sat in.

"This is a disaster," I mumbled to myself.

I wanted to shout, to get everyone's attention and say that under no circumstance should they start looking for work they would prefer. I had visions in my head of half the staff leaving and never coming back a few weeks before our busiest time of year.

But there was nothing I could do. My mouth was too dry, my hands too clammy, and my feet too heavy.

"I can't wait to see what jobs you choose," he said. "And I look forward to meeting each of you properly."

"On your way out," Gia muttered.

I swallowed.

She nudged me. "You have to say something."

I looked over my shoulder at her. "Do you think we could just take down the stupid spreadsheet and quietly dispose of his body?"

"We'll never be able to lift him on our own."

I pursed my lips.

"But Carlos won't ask any questions if I ask for his help."

I smiled. "Thank you for humoring my murderous plan."

"You're welcome," she said. "Would you like me to wear comfortable, disposable shoes tomorrow?"

I shook my head. "That won't be necessary. But only because a missing body would be terrible for business."

"So what are you going to do?"

I folded my arms and watched the staff shuffle out the open double doors into the lobby. "I'm going to ask him what the hell he thinks he's doing."

"Uh-huh."

"And then I'm going to set him straight about how we do business around here."

She squinted. "You mean like how we don't encourage our staff to look for other jobs?"

"Yeah. I'll probably start there."

"Are you going to find three jobs on Monster before you meet with him or-"

"Careful Gia," I said. "There's room for two in a body bag."

She laughed. "You'd never murder me when it's my turn to buy Nino's."

I twisted my mouth. "I suppose I will need a cheesy calzone for strength before I do the job."

"Perfect," she said. "Because I'd love for that to be my last meal."

I checked my watch. "Seven thirty sound alright?"

She nodded. "My place or-"

"Definitely your place," I said, knowing I'd feel even guiltier about avoiding my mom with a bag full of Nino's takeout in hand.

"Sounds good," she said, her brown eyes floating past me. "And good luck with the boss."

"Thanks," I said. "I'm going to need it."

TWELVE
- Adam -

I was checking in with the CFO of Backpack & Craic when Jolie stormed into the office.

"I'm going to have to call you back, Cody," I said, closing my laptop.

"Sure thing," he said. "I'll be here for the rest of the day."

I hung up the phone and looked over the desk to where Jolie was standing with her arms folded. "Not much of a knocker, I take it?"

She raised her eyebrows. "Are you asking whether I feel obligated to knock when I come in my own office?"

"Are you implying you actually spend any time in here?" I asked. "Because I think we both know that's a load of crap."

"I'm better suited to work front of house."

"I don't disagree, *Boss*, but you probably should've brought someone in to manage the books- oh, I don't know- two and a half years ago."

She glanced at the floor to ceiling stack of filing boxes. "My dad used to manage the books."

"Well, unfortunately, they still need managing."

She cocked a hip. "You won't get any points around here for telling people what they already know."

"Great," I said. "So you won't mind that I've hired someone to be your internal numbers guy."

She furrowed her brow. "You hired someone?"

"I did."

"That's a surprise," she said, stepping between the chairs in front of my desk.

"Why?"

"Because I think you made it pretty clear at the staff meeting earlier that what you're really interested in is laying people off."

I tilted an ear towards her. "What would give you that impression?"

She squinted at me. "The fact that you told everyone to look for work?"

I groaned and leaned back in my chair. "First of all, I don't have to explain myself to you."

"I think you do," she said, walking up to the edge of the desk. "It was one thing for you to bust in here and say you want to change the décor and the menu, but it was a step too far making everyone fear for their jobs."

"I'm happy to explain myself," I said, swiveling to one side as I kept my eyes on her. "As a courtesy to you."

"Good becau-"

"But I have to be honest, I'm getting really fucking sick of you not giving me the benefit of the doubt."

"I'm listening," she said, leaning forward and splaying her hands on the desk.

"A black bra, huh?"

She straightened up immediately and checked her shirt.

"You going out after work or is that just for me?"

Her face turned bright pink. "You're disgusting, you know that?"

"Hey," I said, lifting my palms. "You're the one that flashed your boss."

"I did no such thi-"

"You want answers about the job search assignment?" I asked.

"Yeah, I do."

I stood up. "First of all, I'm assuming you didn't take issue with the fact that I said I wanted to get to know everyone?"

"Obviously not," she said. "If anything, I thought that was the most sensible thing you've said since you arrived."

I nodded.

"But then you went and ruined it by acting like some people's meet and greet might also be their last goodbye."

I licked my teeth. "Well, that was never my intention."

"Exactly what was your intention?"

"To be frank, it's an exercise I actually hope will boost morale."

"I'm not following."

"Did you know Debbie worked as an events coordinator for fifteen years?" I asked, walking around the desk.

"Debbie at the bar?"

"Yeah."

"No, I didn't know that," she said, turning around as I took a seat in one of the smaller chairs on her side of the desk.

"Did you know Maria-"

"Housekeeping Maria or lifeguard Maria?"

"Housekeeping."

"What about her?" she asked.

"Did you know she trained as a professional pastry chef in Mexico before she came to this country?"

"No."

I could tell by the look on her face that the last thing she was expecting was for me to know something about her staff that she didn't.

"What's your point?" she asked.

"My point is that I've no intention of firing anyone," I said. "I just want to make sure that no one's underlying passions are being ignored if they could be an asset."

She pressed her lips together.

"And if there are skills that people want an opportunity to learn- regardless of whether they might help them elsewhere or at this job- I want to empower them to build those skills as best I can."

Her shoulders relaxed with her next breath.

"Because I'm well aware that not everyone has been as lucky as you and me."

"I'm listening," she said, leaning back against the desk.

"We grew up with ambitious, supportive fathers who mentored us, encouraged us, and helped us develop into capable business people. And if I can offer even a fraction of similar support to someone else, I would consider it both a pleasure and a privilege."

"I see."

It was odd to see her so speechless. "Do you feel better now?"

"I do," she said.

"You're satisfied that I'm not out to fire your family?"

"Yes."

"Good," I said. "Because I can't fly this thing without you."

Her mouth twitched, and I felt satisfied that she got my meaning.

"That being said, now that I have your attention-" I folded my hands in my lap. "You know what I could do without going forward?"

She wrapped one hand around the back of her neck. "What?"

I stood and stepped up to her. "The fact that you've decided I'm some kind of monster when you were actually quite smitten with me that last summer we spent time together."

"You mean the summer after which I never heard from you again?"

I edged into her personal space and took a deep breath. She smelled like crisp sunshine and fresh linen. "That's irrelevant," I said, searching her eyes. "What matters is that I never forgot this place, and I sure as hell never forgot you."

"I'm flattered, Adam, but-"

"I didn't just come back here for the hotel, you know."

She blinked at me.

My eyes dropped to her glossy lips.

"Well, you're my boss now," she said, her voice soft. "So none of that stuff we did before is ever going to happen again."

"Yes it is."

"Excuse me?"

"It's inevitable," I said, raising my eyes back to hers. "Trust me. The only thing more intense than how bad you still want me is how bad I still want you."

She shook her head so slightly it was almost undetectable.

"And I think we both know I'm the kind of guy who gets what he wants," I said, leaning against her so she could feel her own heat bouncing off me. "Besides, you're-"

"What am I?" she asked, her body still as a startled bunny.

"Desperately in need of a good fuck."

Nervous laughter spilled from her lips. "This is sexual harassment, Adam."

I reached around and grabbed her ass, pulling her against my hard on as I moved to whisper in her ear. "Not if you like it, it's not."

When I heard her breath leave her body, I dragged my lips lightly from just under her ear to her throat.

Then I let her go... so she could think about it.

FLASHBACK
- Adam -

I'd watched her all night from across the room as she cleared and set tables while my family and I focused on getting our money's worth from the Harmony Bay Buffet.

"How was the Skype session with your math tutor?" My dad asked between bites of rump roast.

"Fine," I said. "I'm ahead of schedule apparently."

"That's my boy," my mom said, tousling my hair even though she knew I hated that. After all, I was going to be in high school come fall. God forbid she did that at the school gates. I recoiled, hoping she'd get the message.

Her eyes drooped. "Do you want me to cut your steak?"

"Only if you're going to chew it up for me, too," I said.

"Adam's right, Annette," my dad said. "Besides, you've barely eaten a thing yourself."

"It's because I've been talking too much."

"Not at all, Mom," I said, sawing at my steak. "I thought that stuff about dolphin migration was really interesting."

She smiled at me.

My dad raised another bite. "Beats you filling us in on the latest General Hospital gossip, anyway."

"You guys are too hard on me," she said. "If you aren't more patient, I'm going to bring my sister down next time."

"That will be fun for the two of you," my dad said. "Because, rest assured, I won't be subjecting myself or my son to that much estrogen."

"It's very common to take those pills," my mom said. "But obviously I never should've confided in you."

I furrowed my brow. "What pills?"

"Your Aunt Cathy takes special pills to keep her body hair in check," my dad said.

"That is not what they're for, Ted." My mom turned to me. "She takes pills to balance out her hormones so she doesn't have mood swings."

"Like last Christmas?" I asked.

"Exactly," my dad said.

My mom raised her eyebrows. "You must never tell her you know that."

"I'm pretty sure it's not going to come up."

"Good," my mom said.

"Isn't that your little friend over by the dessert table?" my dad asked, nodding behind me.

I looked over my shoulder and then down at my plate where some tepid mashed potatoes had turned the color of steak juice.

"Go on," my dad said. "She might want to go halves on a slice of pie."

I smiled. Unlike my mother, Jolie wasn't the kind of girl that needed help with a piece of pie. "Are you guys going to the tiki bar after this?" I asked.

"For a quiet one," my dad said, pulling his keycard out of his pocket and tossing it across the table. "We'll meet you back at the room later."

I shoved the key in my pocket and headed towards the dessert table. "Hey," I said, picking up a small plate. "What's good?"

"I like the carrot cake," Jolie said, her eyes bouncing around the desserts.

I scrunched my face.

"But you'd probably prefer the brownies."

I put a few on my plate. "You want to have dessert with me?"

"I can't stay in here," she said. "Staff aren't supposed to eat in front of the guests."

"Outside's cool with me."

She smiled and led the way, turning down a long hallway and leaving through a set of emergency exit doors.

"Where are we?" I asked as my eyes adjusted to the darkness outside.

"Behind the pool house."

I looked around and tried to get my bearings.

"Hold this," she said, handing me her plate.

I watched as she hoisted open the lid of a gigantic plastic crate. Then she threw a leg over the side and jumped in.

I looked over the edge when I heard the squidgy squeaks of whatever she landed on, discovering the resting place of the colorful pool noodles that littered the deck during the day.

I furrowed my brow. "What are you doing?"

"I like to look for shooting stars while I eat dessert."

"From the noodle tub?"

She shrugged. "No one ever bothers me here. Besides, it's comfortable. You'll see."

I handed our plates to her and set my hands on the edge of the tub. "Are they all wet?"

"A little," she said. "But it's only water."

I twisted my mouth and swung my legs over the edge, landing on my side in the noodle pit. The impact of my landing made Jolie fall back on her butt, but somehow she managed to keep our dessert plates level.

I couldn't help but think it was the silliest thing I'd ever done, and I envied the fact that she seemed to think nothing of it. It was one of the first times in my life that I realized there were different kinds of ways to be rich.

We laughed at the funny noises we made as we got settled on the noodles, and by the time we each laid back with our plates in hand, I was struggling to catch my breath.

"What do you think?" she asked when we'd finally settled down.

"It's no treehouse," I said. "But it is comfy."

"Told you."

"Do you ever see any shooting stars?" I asked, staring at the sky as I popped half a brownie in my mouth.

"Sometimes," she said. "But I imagine even more of them."

"What do you mean you imagine them?"

"I mean if you stare at the sky long enough, you start to see things that aren't there."

I finished my brownies quickly and wedged my empty plate between two noodles by my feet. Then I laid back and put my hands behind my head.

"Close your eyes for a second," Jolie said, turning onto her side.

I squinted at her. "Why?"

"Just do it."

"Okay," I said, squeezing them shut. Suddenly I could hear the surf lapping rhythmically in the distance and the wind rustling the sea oats on the dunes.

"Now open your mouth."

"No way," I said through clenched teeth.

"Do it or I'll never talk to you again."

I opened my mouth instantly as I was too young to know that women don't always mean what they say. A moment later, something cakey fell against my tongue.

I opened my eyes as I chewed it, enjoying the sweet, creamy taste of the icing and the feeling of having her shiny eyes trained on me.

"What do you think?" she asked.

"Carrot cake?"

She nodded.

"I think it's so good I could kiss you," I said, my eyes dropping to her mouth.

She licked her lips. "Do you want to?"

"Do you want me to?" I asked.

"You're not supposed to ask."

I lifted my head. "I only did because you did first."

She groaned and rolled onto her back. "The moment's passed."

I rolled onto my side, put my fingers against her far cheek, and turned her face towards me. "So let's have a new moment."

She raised her eyebrows, her hair falling in waves over the colorful noodles under her head as she blinked up at me.

"And this time I won't ask."

Then I kissed her softly on her pink lips, which were grainy with traces of sweet icing, before opening her mouth with mine and swirling my sugar coated tongue around hers.

When I finally came up for air, I licked my lips and stared at her blissful expression.

And when she opened her eyes, they were full of shooting stars.

THIRTEEN
- Jolie -

I wanted to tell Gia what happened in the office, but I wanted to keep it a secret more.

For one thing, I didn't want to admit that I'd let our boss touch me like that.

After all, I hadn't stopped him. I just let him press his dick against me, squeeze my ass, and breathe on my neck.

Even now, just thinking about how lightly he dragged his lips across my skin gave me chills.

At the time, I'd wanted nothing more than to close my eyes, tilt my hips right back against his, and forget that he was my boss, forget that I couldn't have him, forget that letting him make me vulnerable put my dad's entire legacy in jeopardy.

Instead, I froze. My heartbeat stopped, my lungs collapsed, and there wasn't a single coherent thought in my head.

It was as if being that close to him made me forget everything except the most feminine parts of me, the parts I'd been neglecting most these days.

How dare he say I needed a good fuck?! As if he were the man for the job?!

For all he knew, I was having tons of sex outside work hours. Tons and tons. It's not like he'd had the decency to even ask about my personal life before he touched me the way no stranger should touch another.

Not that it felt strange.

On the contrary, it felt torturously good.

I just hoped my sexual frustration wasn't as obvious to everyone else.

God knows what the hell I would've said if he'd asked-like a normal person- if I was seeing anyone? It would've been impossible to make my recent adventures in dating sound even moderately exciting.

I couldn't even convince myself I'd ever met a man half as intriguing as Adam. How on Earth could I have fooled him?

Even growing up, I never thought any of the boys in school were as interesting as the strange boy from the North with the funny accent, the one who was always happy to see me and never treated me differently because I worked at the hotel.

It was like he could see past that, like he could see me better than anyone. It fucked me up for years believing he was one of a kind.

And nothing had changed.

Except now he had the upper hand, and I had everything to lose.

"How many is that?" I asked, tilting another slippery nipple down my throat.

"Does it matter?" Gia shouted over the music.

I tried to look at my watch, but there were too many hands on it for me to make out the time. "Isn't it a bit early to have lost track of how many drinks we've had?"

"It's fine," she said. "We had a big dinner."

My mind flashed back several hours to the calzones. I'd managed over half of mine. "Oh yeah," I said. "Never mind. I don't know what I was worried about."

"Too much," she said.

"What?"

"That's what you're worried about. Too much."

I rolled my eyes. "Somebody has to worry."

"Not on Saturday night!"

"Mmm."

She bumped her shoulder into mine. "You have to let loose and stop trying to control every little thing."

"Easier said than done," I mumbled, reaching for my mojito. "Is this a double?" I asked, sipping from the straw.

She glanced at hers before looking back at me. "I can't remember."

I shrugged. Whatever it was, it was working, and I could feel my stress and inhibitions evaporating into the open air.

"Have you thought about whether or not you want to go to Brian's sister's thing?" she asked, dancing in place with her drink.

I scrunched my face. "I don't know."

"It'll be fun," she said in a sing song voice.

"He'll be so drunk when we get there, though," I said, remembering his sister's last party. "He'll be all handsy, and he'll say cringey stuff to me."

"Yeah." She nodded. "That's horrible when a guy likes you and actually wants to touch you and whisper sweet nothings in your ear. I can't think of anything more awful."

I cocked my head. "You know what I mean."

"Totally," she said. "We should call your ex instead. That way you can spend the rest of the night feeling degraded while he looks past you at other girls. Sound better?"

"You're making me sound like a bitch."

She dropped her chin. "I don't think you're a bitch. I just think Brian's a nice, convenient fuck, and you could use one."

I shook my head. "You don't care about me at all. You're just horny, and you know Carlos is going to be there wringing his hands and watching the door until you show up."

"So what if I am?" she asked. "And what's so bad about hooking up with a guy that can't believe his luck?"

"Nothing. I'm sure it does wonders for his self-esteem."

"And mine," she said. "Last time he called me his pequena diosa?"

I raised my eyebrows.

"It means beautiful goddess," she said.

"You mean little goddess?"

"Whatever," she said, waving my comment away with her hand.

To be honest, I admired the fact that she could be such a guy about it, but treating sex that way was difficult for me. Sure, I'd had more casual encounters than I cared to remember, but they always left me feeling like shit.

I knew it was because I'd been hooking up with people that I didn't have a genuine connection with. And while the mechanics of sex were enough to keep my mind off that sad fact while it was happening, it was the feeling that came the next morning that I was keen to avoid.

It was an empty, used feeling, and it made me feel disposable. What's more, it made me feel like I was farther away than ever from finding someone I might actually have a connection with.

Of course, I knew what Gia meant about Brian being a safe bet. It was nice to feel like a goddess and know that the person you spread your legs for wasn't going to take you for granted, but I didn't need to make some half decent guy's night to boost my own self-esteem.

I wanted to sleep with someone who made it hard for me to believe my luck, too. Was that so much to ask?

"Well you should come anyway," she said. "Maybe there'll be someone else there who'll catch your eye. Lord knows you aren't going to come across any new faces here."

I nodded. "You do have a point there."

"And I don't really care whether you give Brian another go," she said. "But if you don't meet someone soon, you're going to get so backed up you're liable to slip up and shag the boss."

"I'm not going to do that," I said, wondering who I was trying to convince. "Of all people, he's the last guy on Earth I would fuck right now."

"Sorry," a familiar voice said behind me. "I couldn't help but overhear-"

I turned around to see Adam leaning against the bar.

His crisp white shirt and smile glowed in the dim light. "And I'm dying to know who the unlucky guy is."

FOURTEEN
- Adam -

"Hello, Mr. Darling," Gia said. "Can I buy you a drink?"

Jolie shot her a look.

"I was just going to ask you the same question," I said. "My friends and I actually have a table over there, and we've got more champagne than we can drink-"

"Champagne's too sweet for me," Jolie said.

Gia raised her eyebrows. "It wasn't too sweet for you last New Year's when you-"

Jolie slid her foot from her shoe and pressed it down on Gia's toes. "Besides, it wouldn't be appropriate to have a drink with you, seeing as how you're the boss and all."

First Love

"My apologies," I said, fixing my eyes on Jolie. "I thought we were done being appropriate."

"We're not."

"Jolie told me what you're planning with the job search assignment," Gia said. "And I just want to say I think it's really cool."

I smiled. "Well I look forward to meeting with you in the coming weeks, Gia. Something tells me you're a woman of many talents."

"Are you hitting on her now, too?" Jolie asked.

"I'm not hitting on anyone," I said. "I'm merely being polite, which is more than I can say for you."

Her shiny lips twisted into a pout.

"Can I ask you a personal question?" Gia asked, leaning past her friend.

I nodded. "Of course."

"Whatever happened to your friend Christophe?"

Jolie reached for her drink and drained it.

"He's a lawyer now," I said. "In New York City."

Gia nodded. "Still getting into trouble?"

I shrugged. "He hasn't changed much if that's what you're asking."

"Tell him I say hello next time you're talking to him," she said. "If you think he'd remember me."

"I'm sure he remembers you," he said. "You made his summer if I recall."

Gia blushed.

Jolie fixed her eyes on me. "So you were sick of being the third wheel with your friends and decided you'd rather be the third wheel with us, is that it?"

I looked over my shoulder. Carrie was staring at her glass of champagne, her eyes sparkling as Ben whispered in her ear.

"They're sweet," Gia said.

"Yeah," I said, turning back around. "Love happens, I guess. If you're open to it."

Jolie leaned forward and spoke in my ear. "Stop trying so hard. I'm not attracted to you."

"Stop lying to yourself," I whispered back. "It's unbecoming."

"You know this is the seedy locals bar, right?" Gia asked. "You'd probably be happier at one of the clubs in the city."

"I don't know," I said. "I like this place. Why travel when there are drinks and attractive women right here?"

Gia smiled.

Jolie waved down the bartender.

"Anyway, the offer's there if you care to join us," I said, turning back towards my table.

Unable to help myself, I glanced back over my shoulder just in time to see Jolie watching me walk away. When I caught her looking, she turned towards the bar and fumbled for her wallet.

"You guys are going to get us kicked out if you don't keep the PDAs in check," I said, scooting into the round booth.

"Aww," Ben said, turning to me. "Are you feeling left out?" He scooted to my side of the booth and leaned into my personal space. "I can share some sweet nothings with you, too, if you-"

I raised a palm between his face and mine. "That's quite alright."

"Good," he said, scooting back over to Carrie and putting his arm around her. "Because it's nothing personal, man, but Carrie looks a lot better on my arm than you do."

"Agreed."

"What did they say?" Carrie asked, tilting her head towards Jolie and Gia.

"They think you guys are sweet," I said, topping up my glass.

"No," Carrie said. "About coming over?"

"They're thinking about it," I lied.

"Your wifey playing hard to get?" Ben asked.

"She's not my wifey," I said. "And yes. Very hard."

"She's gettable," Carrie said, taking a sip of her champagne. "I wouldn't lose hope yet."

I raised my eyebrows. "First of all, no one said anything about losing hope. Second of all, what makes you think she's gettable?"

Carrie shrugged. "I just saw how her body language changed when she saw you."

"And?"

"She got tense all over like she can't even breathe when you're around."

Ben scrunched his face. "That doesn't sound like a good thing."

"It is," she said. "Besides, willpower is a muscle."

"What's your point?" I asked.

"My point is, she can't fight her attraction to you forever," she said. "She'll get tired eventually."

"And that's when you pounce," Ben said.

Carrie shot him a look. "No. No pouncing. She's not prey."

Ben smiled. "She might as well be for how she makes Adam's mouth water."

I shot him a look. "That's enough. They'll never join us if they sense we're talking about them."

"How about Ben and I go for a dance," Carrie said. "Then, when they notice you're alone, they'll feel bad for you and come over."

"Sounds pretty tragic," I said.

"And if they don't notice?" Ben asked.

Carrie cocked her head. "Then maybe I'm wrong and they genuinely despise you."

I groaned. "Go on, then. I suppose I'd rather know the truth."

"Good luck, buddy," Ben said, sliding out of the booth.

I watched them disappear onto the dance floor, feeling as happy for them as I was jealous of what they had.

It wasn't that I didn't enjoy being a bachelor. I adored my freedom, and I'd unapologetically enjoyed all the perks that came with it for years.

But I also knew that I was ready for something more.

I was ready to find a woman who I wasn't only interested in fucking senseless, but one I might also give a Sunday night foot rub to.

And I loved fine dining as much as the next foodie, but I wanted to be able to open a nice bottle of wine at home and have someone to share it with.

I wasn't sick of going to parties or anything, but the more time I spent with coupled up friends, the more I realized I was missing out on things that were far more substantial. Like inside jokes and kisses goodnight and always having someone to enjoy the little things with.

But I didn't want those things with just anyone. Otherwise I would've bitten the bullet and made an honest woman out of Victoria already.

I sighed and pulled my phone out. It was almost ten o'clock, and I wasn't even buzzed.

I slid the champagne from the ice bucket, figuring I'd have one more glass and go, but just as I was topping myself up, two curvy figures appeared beside the table.

"Still need help with that?" Gia asked, dangling two empty champagne glasses in one hand.

"Please," I said, scooting in.

Gia sat down across from me, and when Jolie gestured for her to scoot in, she refused and nodded to my side of the table.

I could see in Jolie's eyes that she was farther along than the rest of us, but she still managed to lower herself into the booth quite gracefully, albeit reluctantly.

I'd just filled their glasses when Gia pulled her phone out. "Sorry," she said, mostly to Jolie. "I have to take this." Then she yelled "hello" and "one second" into the phone and excused herself, leaving a very drunk Jolie in my company.

FIFTEEN
- Jolie -

Before I could object, Gia had already excused herself, leaving me alone with nothing but a booming blood alcohol level and the one delicious thing I was determined to resist.

"You did a good job back there," Adam said, tilting his head towards the bar.

"What are you talking about?" I asked.

"The way you didn't throw yourself at me in front of your friend," he said. "It was very convincing."

"Give it a rest." I tilted some champagne down my throat. The bubbles were light and crisp, and one sip was all it took for me to remember why I'd had such a good New Year's.

He smiled and leaned back in the booth.

"So what happened?" I asked. "Your friends needed a break from your lame come-ons?"

"I don't come on to my friends," he said. "I only come on to women I'm genuinely interested in."

I squinted at him in an attempt to make him less blurry.

"Women like you."

"You just want what you can't have."

He laughed.

"What's so funny?"

He furrowed his brow. "That wasn't a joke?"

"No."

"Oh."

I tilted an ear towards him. "Why would you think it was a joke?"

"Because there's nothing I can't have."

I rolled my eyes. "Were you dropped on your head as a baby or something?"

"Actually, I was always more clever than most... until one summer when I made the mistake of kissing a girl in a noodle box."

I looked down to hide the tangible blush he'd triggered.

"It's only since then that I've been a fool."

"You should get that checked out," I said.

"I don't need to. I already know the cure."

"What is it?" I asked.

"Apparently, the spell will be broken when I kiss the same enchantress that made me an idiot in the first place."

"Shame," I said. "Looks like you're going to be an idiot forever."

"What if I weren't your boss all of a sudden?" he asked. "Would you be more willing to let down your guard?"

I slid my slender glass towards me. "I'm pretty sure nothing good would come out of letting my guard down around you."

"Hmm."

"What?"

He shrugged. "Something tells me your body would disagree."

"For the sake of argument, if the enchantress you spoke of let you kiss her- just to break the curse of your unbearable ignorance- would you stop all this nonsense?"

"What nonsense?"

"You know," I said. "The flirtation and the lusting and the looking at me like I'm a perfectly dressed steak."

"You mean a perfectly undressed steak."

"Yeah. That's exactly what I mean."

"Perhaps," he said. "Why? Would you be more likely to kiss me then?"

I shook my head. "No. I was just curious."

"Do you always get this shitfaced when you go out?"

I craned my neck back. "Excuse me?"

"Is that an unfair question?"

"It is actually," I said, the back of my neck suddenly hot. "And I'm not shitfaced."

He laughed.

"Stop."

"If you can tell me you're not shitfaced without slurring, I might believe you."

I folded my arms and looked around for Gia.

"Have breakfast with me," he said.

"What did you just say?"

He reached for his glass. "I said have dinner with me."

"That's not what you said."

He furrowed his brow. "Isn't it?"

"No. It most certainly is not."

He took a sip of champagne and licked his lips as he set his glass down. "Maybe you're not as drunk as I thought."

"Maybe I'm n-"

"Otherwise you would've just said yes the first time."

"Watch it, Darling. I'm not too drunk to take offense."

"And what about gracefully accepting a dinner invitation with a gentleman?"

I scoffed. "Sorry- are you supposed to be the gentleman in this scenario?"

He nodded.

"I think I'll pass."

"Why?" he asked. "If I were a woman and a relentless, handsome man were dying to wine and dine me, I'd let him."

"Even if he was your boss?"

"Especially if he was my boss," he said. "And thank you for not objecting to my slipping handsome in there."

"Oh don't get me wrong. I definitely object. I'm just beginning to realize that I have to pick and choose my battles with you."

"Carlos will be here in five," Gia said, sliding into the booth. "I'm so sorry," she said to Adam. "But we sort of had other plans after this."

"What plans?" he asked.

"Just a house party," I said.

Gia fixed her eyes on me. "Would you rather stay here?"

I cocked my head. "It's a little too late for you to ask now."

"I can make sure you get home if you want to stay," Adam said to me.

"I bet you can," I said, not meeting his eye. "But my friends are expecting me."

"Are you sure?" he asked. "Because you've had a lot to drink and-"

I turned to him. "Stop acting like my fucking babysitter. I'm absolutely fine."

Gia turned to Adam. "You can come if you want. Carlos is bringing his truck so it'll be a tight squeeze but-"

"No he can't," I said. "He couldn't abandon his friends like that."

"Yes I can," Adam said. "A house party sounds like fun."

I put my head in my hands.

"In that case," Gia said, "come with me."

I lifted my face as she stood up.

"Stay here," she said to me, pointing at the table like I was a dog who only understood basic hand gestures.

Adam raised his eyebrows at me like he was amused at the whole thing and followed her over to the bar. A moment later, Adam and one of the bartenders walked away together, and Gia joined me back at the table.

"That was amazing," I said. "How did you manage to lose him?"

She furrowed her brow. "I didn't. I just told him he had to swap clothes with Brandon if he wanted to come."

I leaned forward. "What?"

"He can't exactly roll up to a house party looking like he just walked off the red carpet."

I laid a hand across my forehead. "Oh my god I hope you didn't say that to him. That would go straight to his head."

"I didn't," she said. "But you have to admit he totally looks like a celebrity."

"I admit no such thing."

She groaned. "Whatever. Some new digs will sort him out. I'd be so embarrassed if Carlos asked him for gas money or something."

"Why did you even invite him?"

She fingered one of her large hoop earrings. "Because he's my hot new boss that doesn't know anybody, and his friends are too busy sucking face to show him a good time."

"That's not your problem," I said.

"No," she said. "But your sexual frustration is. Besides, now you have options."

"What are you talking about?"

She placed her hands flat on the table. "Don't you see? Now you'll have a chance to see him and Brian side by side and realize what a complete idiot you're being."

"I'm just trying to do the right thing."

"According to who?" she asked. "Your dad? Cause he's not here."

I swallowed. "Obviously I know that."

"Loosen up then," Gia said. "I mean it." She drained half her champagne in one gulp. "Loosen up or go the fuck home."

SIXTEEN
- Adam -

I felt a bit foolish when I realized Gia wanted me to swap outfits with the bartender, but he was so impressed by my clothes I figured what the hell.

"How do I look," I asked, stepping back up to the table.

"Perfect," Gia said.

Jolie's eyes dripped down my tight black t-shirt.

"Give us a spin," Gia said.

I did as I was told and by the time I was facing them again, Jolie's cheeks were pinker than I'd seen them yet.

"Let's wait outside," Gia said.

Jolie knocked her drink back, and I let the girls lead the way.

When Carlos pulled up outside the bar a few minutes later blasting music I hadn't heard for ten years, I had high hopes for the night.

Unfortunately, his narrow backseat was filled with an array of crap that seemed to have no more coherence than a garage sale so we all had to pile in the front. Gia climbed in first, taking the middle seat, and after Jolie and I forced our way in, she was practically sitting in my lap.

"I'm really sorry about this," she said, her fragrant hair falling in my face every time we took a left hand turn.

"Don't worry about it," I said, forbidding myself to get turned on.

"Would it be okay if we pretend you're not our boss?" Gia asked. "I don't want other people to feel like they have to censor themselves around you or-"

"I do," Jolie said. "I want people to feel that way."

"Can't I just be a childhood friend in from out of town?" I asked. "That's not even a lie."

"I'm cool with that," Gia said.

Jolie groaned.

Carlos drummed the steering wheel and sang along to the radio with an endearing level of enthusiasm.

Luckily for me, it only took fifteen minutes to get to the party, which was great because having Jolie in my lap in her short black skirt was making it too easy to forget I was her boss.

"I need a drink," she said, scrambling out of the car when we arrived.

I got out and followed her up to the house. "So is there a special occasion I need to be aware of?" I asked, feeling naked without the obligatory bottle of wine that I would normally bring to a house party.

"It's Brian's sister's birthday," Gia said. "She's 21."

I furrowed my brow. "Shouldn't the party be at a bar then?"

"Why?" Jolie asked. "It's not like it's her first drink."

Carlos pushed the door open, and I was instantly hit by the smell of beer and sweat.

It didn't take me long to realize that a lot of the other guests were practically jail bait and that Jolie was a lot drunker than she'd been when we left the bar.

"I normally bring something to parties like this," I said as I closed the door behind us.

"Oh don't worry," Gia said, waving a hand as she weaved through the crowd. "Carlos has whatever you need."

"No- I mean like a bottle of wine or something."

"No need," she said. "Just make sure you chip in for the keg."

The prospect of a keg made me feel like a student again.

"Jolie!" The skinny blond guy manning the keg put his arms in the air and waved at her.

She forced her way through the cramped kitchen and gave him a hug.

He planted his lips on her cheek so her soft hair fell around his face, and I found myself wishing we were still squished in the car.

The guy seemed set on keeping his arm hooked around her neck but she wriggled free, pulled two cups from the stack, and nodded towards me.

Brian- I gathered- lifted his eyebrows in my direction and filled her cups first, ignoring the other people shoving around him.

Jolie lifted the cups in the air and headed towards me. I met her halfway.

"Did you see where Carlos and Gia went?" she asked, handing me a full Solo cup.

"Thanks," I said, taking my beer and nodding towards the open back door. "I think they went outside."

Jolie turned around and made a beeline for the fresh air, which actually felt cool compared to the sticky air in the house.

From the back porch, I noticed Gia and Carlos sitting at a picnic table in the yard.

"They're over there," I said, touching Jolie gently on the back.

She turned towards them, stepped off the porch, and kicked off her shoes so she could make her way through the grass.

Carlos moved something behind his back when we approached and waved his free hand in front of his face.

"It's okay, Carlos," I said, taking one look at Gia and knowing what they were up to. "Feel free to carry on."

Gia squinted at me through red eyes. "Are you sure you're cool with it?"

I shrugged. "It's none of my business how you unwind."

Carlos nodded approvingly and handed her the joint.

Jolie sat on the bench as if she were sidesaddle on a horse.

I walked around opposite her and took a seat next to Carlos.

"So are you and Brian a thing?" I asked, taking a sip of beer.

She swiveled around and looked at me. "What's it to you?"

"Just curious," I said. "He's obviously into you."

"He wishes he were into me," she said, staring down at her cup.

"I see."

Gia held the joint out. "Want some?"

I lifted a palm between us. "I'm good, thanks."

"Jolie?" she asked, raising her eyebrows.

For a second, I swear she looked at me to see how I would react. And while I didn't think there was anything sinister about enjoying the occasional joint, I knew she was drunk enough that weed would only cut her good time short.

"Yeah, sure," she said, reaching for it.

My lips fell apart, but I knew voicing my concern would only piss her off and make her drag on it even harder.

She kept her eyes on me as she puffed it. Then she handed it back to Gia before blowing the smoke in my direction. Halfway through exhaling, she started coughing her ass off.

"Oh shit," Carlos said. "That's gonna get you." He finished the joint and stomped it out in the grass. "What do you want to drink, babe?" he asked Gia.

"I'll come with you," she said. "I want to say hi to the birthday girl before I get too shitty." Gia stood up and put her hand on Jolie's shoulder. "You going to stay here?"

She nodded.

"Call me if you need anything."

"Yep," Jolie said, dragging out the word.

Gia pointed at me. "Keep an eye on her. She never smokes."

"I'm fine," Jolie said, putting her elbows on the table.

"Thanks for letting me tag along," I said after Gia walked away. "I hope I'm not cramping your style too much."

Jolie sighed. "I'm actually glad you're here."

I raised my eyebrows. "You are?"

She nodded. "I'd rather talk to you than any of these people."

"Color me flattered."

She pointed at me. "Don't let that go to your head."

I lifted my hands. "Of course not."

She raised her beer and then, thinking better of it, set it back down. "I'm really embarrassed to be this fucked up in front of you."

"Don't be."

Her glazed eyes flitted up at me. "I don't want you to lose respect for me just because I had a few too many slippery nipples."

I laughed. "You'd have to behave a lot worse than this to disappoint me, Jolie. Don't worry about it."

"Maybe you should drink faster and catch up," she said. "So you can feel like you're on a teacup ride, too."

I scrunched my face. "You have the spins?"

She squinted and pinched two fingers together. "Little bit."

"We'll stay out here in the fresh air then."

"Is that okay?" she asked.

"Of course."

"Did you mean what you said before?" she asked.

"Can you be more specific?"

She twirled the long string of beads around her neck. "About the enchantress and the kiss and the cure?"

"What are you asking me?"

"Did you really drag your ass all the way down here just so you could kiss me again in the noodle box?"

I laughed. "I want to kiss you in a lot more places than the noodle box."

She glanced down at her lap.

"Why do you ask?"

"That's not okay," she said, lifting her face. "For you to say things like that."

"I wish I could tell you I was sorry," I said. "But I've always felt that honesty was the best policy."

"I have a job to do," she said. "People look up to me. I can't just sleep with you like we're seventeen again."

"That's fine. To be frank, I expect it'll be even better than it was that summer." God knows I was eager to prove to her that I wasn't a bumbling amateur anymore.

"There you go acting like it's definitely going to happen again," she said. "Stop doing that."

I sighed. "Fine. But I can't promise I'm going to stop liking you or stop being attracted to you."

"How is that even possible? I've been nothing but a bitch to you since you arrived."

"I'm afraid my tolerance for difficult women might surprise you."

"Whatever," she said, crossing her arms. "I'm not going to kiss you. So if that's why you came here tonight-"

"Relax. I'm not going to try anything." She was way too drunk. Besides, when it finally happened, I wanted her to actually remember it.

I turned our conversation to some lighter topics- paddle boarding, stupid shit I did in college, what I remembered about the hotel all those years ago- and she loosened up even more, her eyes sparkling as she laughed and nursed her beer.

But by midnight I could tell she was sleepy, and when I asked around, I got the sense that Carlos and Gia were busy having their own party for two.

So in the end, while it wasn't exactly the way I imagined it, I did get to take her home.

S E V E N T E E N
- Jolie -

If the dull throbbing in my head was anything to go by, I wasn't quite ready to open my eyes.

I kept them squeezed shut and rolled over, pulling the comforter up and tucking it tightly around my neck as I curled into a ball.

That's when I realized something was wrong.

The weight of the comforter felt strange. And the pillow beneath my head was odd as well, as if it were downier than usual.

Furthermore, something was digging into my chest. My bra. I was still wearing it... along with my skirt.

My eyes popped open, and I recognized the pale blue wallpaper instantly.

I wasn't at my house. I was in a Harmony Bay Hotel Room.

I craned my neck up over the thick comforter and looked around. The room was virtually empty except for a briefcase on the desk and a phone charger sticking out of the plug on the other side of the bed.

Fuck.

Suddenly, I heard the sound of a room key slip in the door. I scooted back under the covers as quickly as I could and turned my back to the door, leaving my face exposed just enough so I could breathe while I tried to figure out what the hell was going on.

Whatever sleepiness I'd felt moments ago evaporated as I strained to listen to the set of feet moving across the carpeted floor.

A moment later, Adam was standing on my side of the bed with a sheen of sweat coating his rippling abs. "Morning, sleeping beauty."

I was sure then that the pit in my guts would swallow me whole.

"How did you sleep?" he asked, bending over. His dark hair was wet around his face and he was positively glowing.

"Like the dead apparently."

He smiled and walked away.

I sat up, pulling the comforter under my armpits to keep my chest covered. "Do you know where my shirt is?"

He raised his eyebrows and loosened the iPod strap around his muscular arm. "The one you threw in my face last night?"

I swallowed.

He pulled two bottles of water from the mini fridge before heading back over, bending to grab a shirt from the floor on his way. Then he stopped at the end of the bed and tossed one water and my shirt so they landed near the pillows beside me.

I glanced at the other side of the bed as I reached for them, my throat closing up at the realization that we must've slept together.

"You don't remember," he said, his mouth curling into a smile. "There's a shock."

"I feel bad enough right now without you tormenting me."

"I bet you do," he said.

"Under what circumstance did I throw my shirt at you?"

"Well, I never sleep with a shirt on," he said.

"Or exercise apparently," I said, using all my energy to keep from feasting my eyes on the perfect trail of chest hair before me.

"You're sweet to notice," he said, unscrewing his bottle of water. "Anyway, when I took my shirt off last night, you burst out laughing before taking yours off, swinging it over your head, and throwing it in my face."

"Then what?"

"Then I helped you giggle your way into bed where you proceeded to pass out seconds later."

I squinted. "And that's it?"

He cocked his head. "Are you disappointed?"

"Yes," I said. "In myself."

"I'm sure you would've preferred to wake up at home, but I haven't the slightest where you live and it seemed necessary that you have supervision."

"Because you're a pervert?" I asked, pulling my shirt on and yanking it down to where my little black skirt was bunched around my waist.

"I might be a lot of things, Jolie, but I'm not the kind of guy that takes advantage of women who get themselves into a state like that."

"Sorry. I didn't mean to be rude." Lord knows I must've been belligerent because I don't really remember anything after... puffing on that joint. Oh god. Fuck. "I know you were just looking out for me."

"Would you rather I left you at the party?" he asked, setting his empty water bottle on the desk. "Because Brian offered to look after you at least two dozen times."

I bit the inside of my cheek.

"And I like to give people the benefit of the doubt, but I don't think he likes you enough to keep his hands to himself when you're like that."

"That doesn't even make sense."

"It does actually. If you think about it."

My eyes traced the muscles in his back as he spread his legs and stretched for his toes. "What does that say about you?"

He stood up and stretched one arm straight across his chest. "I wouldn't put my hands on you unless it was what you wanted, sober or otherwise."

I hung my head.

"And in my opinion, what a guy wants is no longer relevant once a woman gets in a condition like the one you were in."

I stared at my clasped hands. I didn't want him to think less of me. And I hated thinking about how sloppy I must have been to take my shirt off and dance around his hotel room.

Sure, he could've been lying, but something told me he wasn't. "Where was Gia when you were saving my ass?"

He stretched his other arm across his pecs. "Getting busy upstairs."

I nodded. "I'm so sorry."

"You don't have to apologize," he said, turning around.

My eyes dropped to the way his loose black shorts hugged his ass as he walked into the bathroom.

"I'm just glad I was there to make sure you were okay," he said, his voice bouncing off the tiles.

I dropped my feet to the floor and followed after him. "You know, I appreciate what you did and everything, but I would've been fine even if you hadn't been th-" I froze in the bathroom doorway.

Adam was standing on the rug in front of the sink with his shorts down around his ankles.

I saw everything before it even occurred to me to look away.

He continued reaching for the towel on the rack beside him, unable to hide his amusement at my timing. "You ought to close your mouth before I get the wrong idea."

I hoisted my jaw up from the floor and raised a hand to cover my eyes. "Sorry. Oh my god. I didn't realize-"

"Don't worry about it," he said. "Nothing you haven't seen before."

When I dropped my hand, the white towel was firmly around his hips, just below the sinful v that had led my eyes straight to his cock moments earlier.

"Besides," he said, bending over to pick up his shorts. "For how many times you told me last night that you don't find me attractive, I'm surprised you're blushing at all."

I shook my head. "I'm not sure I could be any more mortified right now if you'd had to hold my hair back."

His eyes shot at me just long enough to make my stomach flip.

"Please tell me you didn't hold my hair back."

"Just the once," he said, plugging his razor into its charger.

I felt my whole body droop.

"But it's no big deal," he said. "Really. To be honest, I was relieved you got sick before the cab ride. As far as I'm concerned, that's the sign of a real champ."

I fell against the doorframe and dropped my forehead against it.

The last thing I felt like was a champ.

EIGHTEEN
- Adam -

I didn't want to pile on when it was obvious that she felt awful, but I also didn't think I'd be doing her any favors by lying.

After all, I wanted her to be more careful in the future. There was no shortage of guys at that party who seemed to be keeping their eyes on her for all the wrong reasons, and the thought of someone hurting her or making her do something she didn't want to do was so upsetting it made me worry that I liked her even more than I realized.

I sat on the edge of the tub and turned the hot water on. At home, I had a much loved Jacuzzi habit. But here, I had to settle for regular baths to ease my muscles.

I could feel Jolie watching me, and the fact that she hadn't fled the scene made me wonder if there was still some alcohol in her system.

"You take baths?" she asked, scrunching her face.

"Sometimes. Why?"

"I would've thought you were a shower guy."

"Because…?"

"Because your time is valuable and all that."

I nodded. "I find the more valuable it becomes, the less apologetic I am about doing what the hell I want with it."

"Understandable."

"There are ways I prefer to unwind," I said, letting her catch me admiring her toned legs. "But it seems this will have to do for now."

She bit her lip.

"And I do try to maximize the time," I said. "By listening to audiobooks or having meetings with colleagues… like this one."

Her eyes grew wide.

"That was a joke, Jolie. I don't hold staff meetings in the tub."

"Right. Obviously. I'm sorry. This is really inappropriate." She ran her fingers through her hair and leaned forward to peek in the mirror, rubbing the smudged eyeliner from under her eyes. "I should go and leave you to your-"

"I disagree," I said, standing. "I think the only thing that's inappropriate is how many clothes you have on right now."

She scoffed. "Do you really think I'm the kind of girl who would fall for this?"

I walked up to her and lowered my voice so it was barely audible over the sound of the roaring water. "Can I be honest?"

"Of course."

"I think you're the kind of girl who's waited her whole life for this."

"You've got me all wrong," she said. "I know I behaved poorly last night, but I don't just give myself to anyone."

"I know you don't," I said, dragging a thumb across her cheek. "But I can assure you, when you give yourself to me, you won't regret it."

She blinked at me.

I dropped my hand and curled the tips of my fingers around the bottom of her skirt where it hugged her thigh. "Because I like you for all the right reasons. I like things about you other people don't even notice."

Her eyes dropped to my lips.

"And it's that attention to detail that's going to make all the difference."

Her bloodshot brown eyes lifted up to mine.

"Maybe I've got you all wrong," I said, dragging my fingertips up over the front of her skirt. "But something tells me you've never been with a real man." I slipped my hand under the bottom of her shirt. "A man who puts your pleasure first." When my fingers grazed her belly button ring, I flattened my palm against her warm stomach. "A man who doesn't stop until you say when."

"When," she whispered.

The knock on the door nearly shocked her out of her skin.

"That must be my room service," I said, pulling my hand back to myself. "Do you want to get that or-?"

"Very funny," she said, flattening herself against the inside wall of the bathroom as if the middle of the room were booby trapped. "Do not say I'm here."

I walked to the door laughing. "Good morning, Anya. How are you today?" I asked as she wheeled in the tray.

"Very good, sir."

"I told you to call me Adam," I said, slipping her a tip.

"Sorry sir."

"Otherwise, I'll have to start calling you ma'am and you're far too young for that."

Anya giggled as she bowed backwards out the door. "Anya is fine, sir- Mr. Adam."

"Just Adam," I said, realizing she probably didn't know where to look as I was in a towel.

She blushed and waved and disappeared.

I closed the door. "Your breakfast is here princess."

Jolie came out of the bathroom like a wary kitten.

"I didn't know if you wanted eggs or carbs so I got both."

"You didn't have to do that," she said.

"I didn't have to carry you to bed last night, either, but I'm an extra mile kind of guy." I lifted the silver domes off the warm plates. "Help yourself. Otherwise it will just go to waste."

While she deliberated over whether she was just going to eye the food or eat it, I went to check the bath. It was nearly full and way too hot to get in, so I turned off the faucet and returned to the breakfast spread.

Jolie was sitting on the edge of the couch, eating a slice of berry covered Belgian waffle with her hands. "I didn't realize how bad I needed this."

"I'm glad I could do something right," I said, sitting in the chair across from her.

"I'm sorry I've been a bitch," she said. "I didn't deserve to have you look out for me last night, and you did it anyway."

"You haven't been a bitch," I said. "You're just trying to make sense of a lot of changes, and you have a huge amount of responsibility. I get that."

"Thank you for being understanding."

I shoved some buttery egg onto a slice of toast and folded it in half. "Does this mean you're prepared to stop bearing your teeth at me all day every day?"

"I'm prepared to do whatever it takes to get you to promise you'll never mention last night to anyone."

I raised my eyebrows. "Careful now. I have a very active imagination."

"Within reason."

I squinted at her and took another bite of my buttery egg sandwich.

"I know I've been unwelcoming, but I crossed the line allowing myself to become a drunken handful." She shook her head. "I always hit the bottle too hard when I'm nervous."

"Nervous? I hope you weren't nervous because of anything I did."

"Of course not," she said. "Anyway, can I count on you to not mention this whole… fiasco to anyone? I mean, it's in both our best interests to create the illusion that things have been nothing but professional."

"Apart from the filthy thoughts you have about me that are written all over your face?"

"That's in your head."

I laughed.

"Seriously," she pleaded. "I'm begging you."

"Have dinner with me," I said. "For your sins."

"Are you sure more time with me is really what you want? I've been a total nightmare."

"I'm sure," I said. "Just dinner. I'll come as not your boss and you can come as... someone pleasant and reasonably sober."

"Ouch."

"What do you say?" I asked. "I think it's a very reasonable request since you said you'd do *anything*."

"If I agree, do you swear you won't say a word to anyone?"

"I swear. Besides our children," I said, flicking the paper cover off my orange juice. "Who I'm sure will find the story hilarious once they're old enough."

"Let's pretend you didn't say that," she said. "And I thought we were talking about dinner?"

"We are."

"Nothing more," she said, lifting her juice.

I nodded. "Nothing more. I assure you I'll behave like a gentleman worthy of the company of a lady like yourself."

"I better not have detected sarcasm there."

"Why don't you just say yes before I decide I want something more inconvenient?"

"Fine," she said, crossing her legs. "But we have to go somewhere far away. I don't want to risk running into anyone we know."

I smiled. "Yeah, god forbid someone sees you out with a loser like me."

"I mean it," she said. "No funny business."

"Fair enough." I extended a hand across the table. "No funny business. Just fun."

NINETEEN
- Jolie -

I didn't want to like the woman whose job it was to change the entire look and feel of the hotel, but she was making it really difficult.

"My only concern with this one," Carrie said, dragging her hand along the back of the soft white couch. "Is that it's too comfortable."

I sat down on the sofa in the middle of the large showroom and crossed my legs.

"And I don't know how much you really want people loitering in the lobby."

"Don't you think the white will get dirty?" I asked, looking over my shoulder at her.

Her long blonde hair was pulled up in a loose bun and she had an actual scarf tied around her neck like she'd just walked out of a Parisian café. "With what? Sand? The weather's so good here it's not like kids are going to be putting muddy boots up on the cushions."

"Mmm."

"Besides," she said, walking around the couch to sit beside me. "White and blue doesn't date."

I knew she was implying that our current sea foam green and cream palate was nauseatingly dated. And while she was right, my dad always liked the green so it felt disloyal to agree with her.

"Furthermore," Carrie continued. "It'll look fabulous on the website."

I raised my eyebrows. "We're changing the website, too?"

"Of course," she said. "Why wouldn't you? That would be like making over a retail store and not changing the shop window."

"I suppose you're right."

"Look," she said, turning to me. "I know it's hard to make so many changes so quickly to what for all intents and purposes has been your home since you were a little girl-"

"So you do get it."

"Of course," she said. "And it can't be easy to trust strangers you don't know to implement those changes, but we're professionals."

"I know."

"So you can trust us."

I nodded.

"I get that this hotel is your life, Jolie. Your baby. But you have to remember that my reputation is on the line, too. And so is Adam's. We wouldn't have taken on the project if we didn't think we could improve on what you have now."

I noticed a couple across the room trying out the handles on a row of standalone doors.

"Him especially."

"What's that supposed to mean?" I asked.

"It means this project isn't just about the money for him."

I tilted an ear towards her. "What else is it about?"

"Oh c'mon. Don't be thick."

I craned my neck back. "It's not about me if that's what you're implying."

"It doesn't have nothing to do with you either."

"Did he say something to you?" I asked.

"He didn't have to," she said, leaning back on the couch, her perfect posture disappearing into the cushions. "It's obvious."

"What is?"

"The fact that he likes you."

"Well, we've known each other a long time," I said, sliding my hands under my thighs.

"I don't think it's that kind of fondness to be frank."

"Did he put you up to saying this?"

"Oh my god no," she flattened a hand across her chest. "He would kill me if he thought I even mentioned it."

"So why are you mentioning it?"

"Because I'm curious what you're thinking," she said. "Since the guy's just about the most eligible bachelor I know."

"I suppose he is more eligible than most."

A woman walked by a nearby chair, looked at the enormous price tag dangling off the back, and kept walking.

"I've tried to set him up with my friends," she said. "But he's very hard to please."

"That's not at all intimidating."

"I don't mean it like that," she said, cocking her head. "I just mean that most women bore him."

"You don't."

She laughed. "He has to put up with me because of Ben."

"How did you two meet?" I asked, desperate to turn the tables so my cards could remain firmly against my chest where they belonged.

"He was my client," she said. "Believe it or not."

"Oh dear. That must've been confusing."

"It was," she said. "And I'd literally just started my own business so I was extra determined to follow the basic rules of good business practice."

"Like don't sleep with your clients?"

"Exactly."

"So how long did you hold out?"

"It's kind of a long story," she said. "I'd just gotten out of a pretty bad relationship, too, so I was sort of a mess."

"Sorry."

"It's okay," she said. "I mean, it wouldn't have been okay if I'd ended up with my ex, but I didn't. And then Ben came along, and I've never been happier."

"Glad to hear it."

"Sorry," she said. "You probably don't even want to know."

"No. It's fine."

She shrugged. "I just couldn't help but notice the way Adam looks at you, and I guess I wish someone had been around when Ben and I first got together to tell me what I was too blind to see."

"I appreciate your concern, Carrie," I said, dropping my head back on what was proving to be a very comfortable couch indeed. "But even if you're right, it's not like anything could come out of it, so it's not worth rocking the boat."

She narrowed her eyes at me. "Why couldn't anything come out of it?"

"Because he's my boss, and he's from a different world."

"What do you mean?" she asked.

"I mean he drinks champagne regularly and probably understands the rules of cricket."

"So?"

"So I drink beer by the bucket and buy my clothes at TJ Maxx."

"I think it's kind of unfair for you to hold it against him that he has money."

I furrowed my brow. "I'm not holding it against him."

"Kinda sounds like you are."

I sighed. "You wouldn't understand."

"Actually, I do understand," she said. "I had the same concern when I started seeing Ben."

"Yeah?"

"And I'm still getting used to it," she said. "But it wouldn't matter if he lost it all tomorrow. What matters is that we're a team."

"I'm happy for you, Carrie. Really, I am. But I don't see what that has to do with me."

"All I'm saying is guys like Adam are hard to come by."

I pressed my lips together.

"So don't let his background intimidate you into overcomplicating everything," she said, rising to her high heeled feet. "At the end of the day, we're all just awkward teenagers looking for a bit of acceptance."

"I get that."

"And I get that it's complicated because he's your boss, but I feel compelled to tell you- from one woman to another- that he's not the kind of guy that chews through women like they're disposable. He's one of the good guys."

"Thanks for the public service announcement."

She smiled. "You're welcome."

"You done?"

"Done," she said, extending a hand to help me up. "Just as soon as we strike a mean deal on this couch."

TWENTY
- Adam -

I suspected she didn't know what she was doing when she pulled her shirt off and danced around in her black lace bra, but I was half convinced she did it just to torture me.

And I couldn't get the image out of my head.

I was shocked at how light she was when I carried her to bed, and the realization filled my mind with filth. There would be no shortage of ways I could enjoy her body, if only she'd entrust me with it.

But she was holding strong, and it had been days since I'd even been close enough to touch her.

Instead, I admired her from afar, watching as the customers fell in love with her and the staff bent over backwards to impress her.

Yes, she was hot. Between her long hair and her toned ass and the way her heavy lashes hung over her brown eyes, there was no way I was the only guy that was attracted to her.

But it was more than that. She had an obvious strength that fascinated me and drew me to her. No matter how far away I managed to get physically, my mind was constantly wondering what she was doing and who might be enjoying her wide smile.

I couldn't fantasize about our teenage exploits forever, though. As vivid as my memories were of pulling down her bikini bottoms and getting my first taste of her to squeezing her nipples and feeling her back arch towards me, it wasn't enough.

I had to have her again, had to hear the moans she only released behind closed doors, had to feel her tan legs wrapped around me as I drove deep inside her.

And if it didn't happen soon, I was going to go crazy.

But breaking down her walls and making her see that I meant her no harm had proved more difficult than I anticipated, and I desperately needed to take a step back and reassess the situation.

Because while I believed that honesty was usually the best policy, my frankness hadn't been enough to convince her that I had nothing but good intentions for us.

As a result, I figured it was about time I solicited a second opinion.

The thought crossed my mind to ask Ben what he thought, but I didn't want to risk him saying anything to Carrie, especially considering how closely she'd been working with Jolie.

Plus, he was so loved up these days he was thinking even less clearly than I was. What's more, he was a diplomat, and what I needed was someone who would give the truth to me straight, no matter how difficult it was to hear.

"Well, well, well," Christophe said when he picked up the phone. "You miss me already, huh?"

I laughed. "Yeah. Lost without you, man. How did you know?"

"It was inevitable," he said. "What's up?"

I leaned back on the bench, watching as happy holiday goers traveled along the boardwalk on their way home from a long afternoon at the beach. "I need some advice."

"Legal or sexual?"

"Neither," I said.

"There's no other kind," he said. "Except for financial, but if you've cocked up the hotel deal that bad already, I'm cutting ties."

"It's about a woman."

"That's what I thought."

I rolled my eyes. "You know how you're always convincing women who are repulsed by you to spend the night?"

"That's not a very friendly question," he said. "And I haven't the slightest what you're talking about."

"Sorry. Let me put it another way." I crossed an ankle over my opposite knee. "You know how you're the master of convincing women to change their initial perception of you?"

"I might know what you're alluding to."

"Good."

"But I'd rather you skip the analysis of my game and acknowledge the fact that you're the one having difficulties."

I groaned.

"You in love or something?"

"I don't know," I said. "It's too soon to tell."

"Because she hasn't realized yet what a fantastic catch you are?"

"I don't appreciate the mocking tone," I said. "But that's not a completely inaccurate way to describe what's happening."

"Let me guess, you laid all your cards on the table already?"

I furrowed my brow. "What do you mean?"

"Have you or have you not admitted to this girl that you're lusting after her?"

I watched as a dragonfly stopped to rest on the bench beside me. "I have."

"What did I tell you about that honesty crap?" he asked. "You can't get away with that shit."

"Bu-"

"Stop pretending you're a regular guy," he said. "You're the only one who actually thinks you're a regular guy."

"That's not true."

"Yes it is. You were born with a silver spoon in your mouth, you've got more money than some countries, and the only reason Christopher Reeve got to play Superman in the movies is because your jawline hadn't been born yet."

"Remind me to call you more often."

"Seriously, Adam, you're not a regular guy. Your family home has a helicopter pad. Get a grip."

"That's what I'm trying to do. What's your point?"

"My point is that you're intimidating, and any women with more than two brain cells to rub together is going to think you're too good to be true if you openly proposition her."

"I don't want to go for dumb women. I want to go for... one woman in particular."

"So cool your jets and don't come on so strong," he said. "Smart women are like cats. They have to suss you out for a bit, and the more you act like you can take them or leave them, the more interested they become in you."

"And dumb women?"

"Dogs all the way," he said. "They'll run right up to you and lick you anywhere you'll let 'em just for showing up."

"Ouch."

"I take it you're after a cat?" he asked.

"Yes. Though for the record, I'm opposed to you reducing women to such disrespectful stereotypes."

"Then you should grow a set, Adam. Because I got laid last night, and something tells me you didn't. So if there's anything you should be offended by, be offended by how light my sack is today."

I pushed my sunglasses onto my head and pinched the bridge of my nose.

"Have I made myself clear?"

I dropped my hand. "I can't suddenly act aloof. She already knows I'm into her."

"That's where you're wrong," he said. "Women are only as secure as their most recent compliment."

I squinted, determined not to miss a word.

"It's never too late to let a woman chill on the back burner."

"And then what?"

"Let her come to you," he said. "Like a cat."

"And if she doesn't?"

He laughed. "Ye of little faith."

"Seriously."

"She will," he said. "Trust me. It's intimidating to be aggressively pursued by someone like you."

"If you say so."

"What you want is for her to be on offense."

I nodded. "I like the sound of that."

"So don't force her into a defensive position."

"That makes sense."

"And for the love of god, don't compliment her immediately every time you see her."

I turned to look at the dragonfly, but it was gone. "Why not?"

"Because that's like giving a dolphin a fish after it's only done one little trick."

"You've been watching too much Animal Planet."

"And eating too much pussy, which is more than I can say for you."

I sighed. "Fair enough."

"Take it from me, the more you pretend not to notice all her little tricks, the more tricks she'll be willing to perform."

"Is it fair to assume you wanted me to read into that?"

He groaned.

"By the way, do you remember the girl you hooked up with when you came down here?"

"Mama Mia Gia," he said. "How could I forget? That girl had swivel in her hips that's illegal in thirty four states."

"Which is even more impressive than the fact that she remembers you."

He scoffed. "Of course she remembers me."

"Just thought you'd want to know."

"You know me so well," he said. "Is she seeing anybody these days?"

"Seeing, yeah," I said. "But from what I gather, it's not any more serious than that."

"How long did you say you were going to be down there?"

"Till the end of the summer," I said. "So if you're looking for a relaxing weekend break-"

"Always," he said. "If only I had a buddy in the area with a hotel."

TWENTY ONE
- Jolie -

I asked him to pick me up at my house because I didn't have a better idea.

I knew I'd feel like a hooker if I met him on a random corner, and I sure as hell wasn't going to loiter around the lobby where everyone would see us leaving... even if I would've been a lot more comfortable on the new furniture there than I was pacing in front of my window.

Fortunately, I knew my mom would be at a bridge tournament with her sister, so there was no risk that she'd look out the window and see me leaving with the man she'd just signed her life's work over to.

Which was good because the situation was stressful enough, especially because I didn't know whether to consider the outing a date or not.

As a result, I had no idea what to wear.

I didn't want to be too dressed up... or too underdressed as I'd been the previous weekend in my black bra and mini skirt. In the end, I'd had no choice but to try on every last thing in my closet and cast the rejects onto the floor.

Finally, I went with white capris and a sheer turquoise shirt, the combination of which made me look really tan.

To dress up the look, I wore some of my nicer jewelry, figuring that wherever he was taking me, my collection of friendship bracelets and concert wristbands would probably look out of place.

Luckily for me, I was so panicked over what I was going to wear that I didn't have time to obsess over all the things he said the morning after Brian's sister's party... all that stuff about me needing a man, his "attention to detail", and how he liked me for things nobody noticed.

Seriously, what did that even mean?

When he finally pulled up in a little red convertible, my eyes rolled so hard I thought they might fall out of my head.

By the time I reached the curb, he'd gotten out and opened the passenger side door.

"Nice whip," I said, getting in.

He closed the door and walked around the front of the car.

I took a deep breath and tried to remind myself that he was just a boy and I was just a girl and we were all just insecure teenagers inside like Carrie said.

Most of all, though, I reminded myself to be pleasant. That was part of the deal, and since he obviously wasn't going to go away, I needed to stop carrying on like a child who believed everything could be solved with a wall of silence.

"Thanks for picking me up," I said.

"Thanks for giving me such good directions."

I glanced at him out of the corner of my eye. He was in navy slacks and a crisp white shirt, looking even more tan than me, and the way his hand gripped the steering wheel sent my mind so far into the gutter I began to wonder how I was ever going to survive the night.

"I thought we'd just grab dinner at the hotel," he said as we pulled up to the first light. "Since seafood buffet night is my favorite."

I glared at him.

He smiled, and I swear if the sun had been higher in the sky, it would've glinted off his teeth.

"Just kidding," he said. "I've made special arrangements in order to respect your reasonable request."

"Thank you."

He nodded.

"So where are we going?" I asked.

"You'll see," he said. "It's a surprise."

"Of course it is."

"What?" he asked. "You don't like surprises?"

"No," I said. "Surprises are fine. I'm just used to small scale surprises like a bread basket I wasn't expecting or a coupon for something I actually want at the grocery store."

"If that's my competition, I feel pretty good."

When a familiar song started to flow out of the speakers, I asked if I could turn it up.

"Of course," he said, reaching for the volume control. "I love this song."

"Me too."

"You like Dire Straits?" he asked. "Or do you just like songs about Romeo and Juliet?"

"Both, I guess." I leaned back and let the wind whip my hair. "My hair is going to be a hot mess when we get wherever we're going."

"Not to worry," he said. "No one's going to see it but me."

I raised my eyebrows. "Is that a clue?"

"Do you want a clue?"

I nodded.

"Then yeah. I suppose that is one."

"Is it a fancy place?" I asked. "Like with a fancy menu?"

He pretended to think about it.

"Sorry," I said. "I realize that was two questions at once."

"The place is fancy, but the menu isn't."

I squinted at him. "What will we drink with dinner at this fancy place with simple food?"

"Wine," he said, leaning back in his bucket seat. "Or champagne."

"Is there entertainment?"

"Not unless you consider my sense of humor entertaining."

"That's a no then."

He laughed.

"Is there any chance I've been there before?"

He pulled up at a stoplight. "Do you really want to count that as one of your questions?"

"Sure, why not?"

He turned to face me. "Because you should know by now that I'm not interested in taking you places you've been before."

I swallowed.

"Does that answer your question?"

I nodded. "How far away is it?"

"Two minutes."

I knew right where we were. There were only two restaurants in the area. One was a seafood place near the pier and the other was the restaurant in the yacht club, but that was only accessible to members. Therefore, when we pulled into the parking lot of the marina, I was fairly sure I'd figured out the surprise.

"You're a member here?" I asked as he parked the car.

"Where?"

"At the yacht club?"

"No," he said, opening his door.

I got out quickly so he wouldn't feel like he had to open mine again. "So we must be going to Sharky's then?"

He walked to the trunk. "I like a hush puppy as much as the next guy, but if you think Sharky's counts as a fancy place, then you're going to be very impressed."

I stepped up to the trunk as he was lifting a cooler out. "We're picnicking?"

"You got me," he said, extending the handle on the cooler before closing the trunk. "Right this way."

I followed him, eager to discover what he was up to, and as he headed for the gate that separated the private boats from the parking lot, I started to get excited.

He punched in a keycode and pushed the gate open for me.

I stepped past him and held it open so he could wheel the cooler by. Then I closed the gate and took a deep breath.

In all my years growing up there, I'd never been on that side of the gate so close to the fancy boats. Even if all we were going to do was look at the boats up close, it would be enough to make my day. But something told me he wasn't the kind of guy that was satisfied with fawning over other people's boats.

I hurried to catch up with him.

"Is this yours?" I asked when he stopped in front of an enormous sailboat. It was white and blue and had Barbara Ann written across the back in fat script.

"No," he said. "It belongs to a family friend."

"I always thought having a friend with a boat would be better than actually owning one."

"You're absolutely right," he said, lifting the cooler over the side of the boat and lowering it onto the deck. "They're a terrible investment and require a huge amount of maintenance."

"I can only imagine."

He pulled the edge of the boat as close to the dock as he could and made a come hither gesture.

I took hold of the small ladder and climbed over the side onto the dock.

"That's why I'm going to put off buying one as long as I can," he said.

"Are we going to take it out or just picnic on it?" I asked.

He bent down and started unwinding the fat ropes from the metal hooks on the dock. "We're going to take it out."

I furrowed my brow. "Who's going to sail it?"

"I am," he said, tossing the rope onto the deck.

"You can sail?"

He nodded. "Where I come from everyone and their little sister can sail."

"Wow."

"It's not a big deal," he said. "Once someone shows you a few simple maneuvers, it's remarkably straightforward."

"I doubt it," I said, convinced there was nothing remarkably straightforward about navigating a boat worth more than most people earn in a lifetime.

Just like there was nothing straightforward about him.

Or what was going to happen tonight.

And for a fleeting moment, I was okay with that, okay with letting go, setting sail, and seeing where the wind- and Adam- might take me.

TWENTY TWO
- Adam -

I could already tell that getting the boat had been worth it. Jolie was clearly going out of her way to not make too big a fuss about it, but more than that, she was obviously enjoying herself.

After I poured us each a glass of chilled white wine, I showed her the best place to sit up at the front while I got us out of the marina. And as soon as the wind hit her face, even I could feel her tension melt away.

The other good thing about putting some distance between us for a few minutes was that it gave me a chance to sail while admiring a beautiful woman, and the combination of my two favorite things meant it had already been a great night.

What's more, it gave me time to remind myself about what Christophe had said.

I hated when he made sense because he was such an idiot, but I thought he made a few good points.

After my conversation with him ended, I tried to imagine what the last few weeks had been like for Jolie. Eventually, I began to understand how my showing up and blatantly lusting after her had become one more thing on her plate as opposed to a welcome surprise.

And if I had to dial it down to make her feel comfortable around me, I was willing to do it. In fact, it frightened me to think about what I might be willing to do to make her happy, to make her see that I wasn't just some Yankee asshole who came down here to flash the cash and swing my dick around.

Every time she turned to look at me from the bow, she had a big smile on her face, and I was pleased to see she was sipping away merrily on her wine. She was truly delivering on her promise to be pleasant, and it meant a lot to me.

For the first time in a long time, I felt optimistic.

After navigating through some strong wind by the shore, I turned up the coast into a gentle current, secured the sail, and went up to the front of the boat to join her.

"You're quite the confident sailor," she said as I sat down across from her.

"Thank you."

"What other skills are you hiding from me?" she asked.

My mouth curled into a smile. "That's confidential."

She rolled her eyes but blushed all the same.

"How are your sea legs?" I asked.

"Fine," she said. "The boat's much steadier than my paddle board anyway, and I get out on that at least a few times a week."

"Of course."

"You should try it sometime."

I shook my head. "I prefer to do things I'm good at to create the illusion that I'm good at everything."

"I'm sure you'd have no trouble," she said. "It's all in your core."

I raised my eyebrows. "You approve of my core, do you?"

"I think your core is excessive."

"To be honest, that's the first complaint I've ever gotten about it."

"It's not really a complaint," she said, pushing some hair out of her face so it blew behind her head. "More like an observation.

"Are you hungry?" I asked. "Is it time for me to dazzle you with a selection of bite size delicacies?"

"Oh yes, please," she said, draining her wine. "And a top up, too, if you don't mind."

"Certainly," I said, handing her my glass. "Finish that off for me, and I'll be right back."

I made my way to the back of the boat and rolled the cooler along the shiny wooden deck.

She crossed her legs. "I'm so excited to see what you brought."

"You like chicken nuggets, right?" I asked as I came to a stop. "And generic ketchup? I thought I'd save some money by not getting the Heinz because the budget brands are just as good-"

"Blasphemy."

"I'm joking," I said, taking a seat. "First things first." I pulled out the wine and topped up our glasses. "I'll take that back from you now," I said, reaching for mine.

"This is really fun, Adam," she said. "Thanks for going to all this trouble."

"It's my pleasure."

"No really. I feel like I'm being rewarded for my bad behavior."

"We both are," I said, lifting my glass.

She clinked hers against mine. "To old friends and new beginnings."

"Oh we're toasting now?" I asked. "I want to make one."

She nodded towards my glass. "Drink to mine first."

I did as I was told. "Yours was perfect so I'll have to take some time to think of a good one myself."

"Of course," she said. "I wouldn't dream of hearing some off the cuff toast now. That would spoil the whole evening."

I smiled. "I'm glad we agree."

"Now for the grub," she said, eyeing the cooler.

I pulled the lid of the cooler straight up so the built in table legs would come out smoothly.

Her face lit up. "Go go gadget table!"

"I'm glad you're impressed," I said, setting it between us. "It was my first successful Kickstarter project."

"Your first what?"

"You know, that website you can use to raise money for new inventions."

She looked between me and the table. "Are you seriously about to tell me you're an inventor?"

"I wouldn't go that far. I've only had two successes and they're really niche."

"What's the other one?"

"It's an amplifier that rolls up."

She craned her neck forward. "An amplifier?"

"Yeah, for people who want to travel light, but also loud."

"Was that a Kickstarter thing, too?" she asked.

"Yeah. It's only been a modest success, but the people who use it seem to like it."

"Do you play guitar?"

"I dabble," I said. "But I'm not good enough to travel with an amp or anything. I only came up with the idea because, when I was eighteen, my dad said I had to quit caddying and get a real job or work with him for the summer."

"So naturally you became an inventor. That's really normal."

I shrugged. "It wouldn't have been any more normal for me to follow my dad around. Besides, I always knew I wanted to be my own boss."

"Wow," she said. "I guess you're not quite as new at that as I thought."

TWENTY THREE
- Jolie -

Maybe I'd been unfair.

When Adam showed up with the deeds to my father's hotel in his pocket, I assumed he was a spoiled little rich boy who was used to taking whatever the hell he wanted from people that couldn't stop him.

And I still thought he was spoiled.

But obviously his fortune hadn't been entirely handed to him. He'd earned at least part of it through hard work and innovative thinking.

Furthermore, he hadn't said he'd always wanted to boss people around. He'd said he wanted to be his own boss, which was something I could identify with, something I could admire.

"I think you've built enough suspense over what's for dinner," I said.

His eyebrows flashed as he reached in the cooler. "For starters, we have fresh crab on crisp toast."

I licked my lips and reached for the plate. "And what will you be having?"

"We also have spicy prosciutto and a selection of cheeses to complement the finest table crackers Food Lion has to offer," he said, laying down the plate of fancy finger food.

"This is the best dinner ever so far."

He set down another colorful plate. "Fresh vegetables with hummus and ranch."

"Did you know I'm obsessed with ranch?"

"Lucky guess," he said, pulling a round Tupperware container from the cooler. "And for dessert, I got a carrot cake."

I smiled. "A carrot cake, huh?"

"I thought I remembered you liked those."

"Good memory," I said.

He fixed his eyes on mine. "All the ones with you in them are."

I felt my cheeks burn against the cool breeze. "This is lovely, Adam. You didn't have to go to so much trouble."

"And you didn't have to give me a chance to take you out," he said. "But I appreciate it."

Little creases sprang around my eyes. He looked so handsome and at home on the boat, and I felt like I could finally let myself appreciate his good looks since I wasn't afraid of being caught out by anyone I needed to be professional in front of.

"The food isn't actually supposed to be the highlight," he said.

"Oh?"

"It was the view I was hoping would wow you."

I swallowed. "Well, you do clean up nice."

"I wasn't digging for compliments there. I was talking about that view," he said, nodding behind me.

I looked over my shoulder and gripped the side of the boat with one hand. The scene before me took my breath away.

In the distance, streams of pink and orange swirled in the sky over the beach. But it wasn't just any patch of sand the warm sunset was shedding light on. It was the Harmony Bay Hotel that was basking in the evening glow.

My eyes watered, and I blinked the tears away before glancing back at Adam and offering him a smile.

I couldn't quite speak yet so I turned back around and looked at the long white building that I'd watched my dad put his sweat and blood and bank loans into so he could make it rise up beside the dunes.

He told me that someday it would all be mine, and even though that dream wouldn't come to pass now, what he'd achieved still amazed me. And I knew then that even if Adam hadn't shown up, it never would've been mine anyway- just like it was never my dad's.

The resort belonged to the people who worked and stayed there, the people who brought it to life, the people whose memories of it played in their minds years after their visit. In reality, it was owned by thousands of individuals, each of whom had a tiny part of it in their hearts and heads.

But due to all the recent excitement, I'd forgotten that. And in that moment I decided I would never allow myself to forget it again.

Because even if the hotel wasn't in my name, it was still his legacy. And the best way for me to honor him would be to keep working my ass off, regardless of whether or not there might ever be something in it for me.

"It's beautiful, isn't it?" Adam said quietly.

I nodded. "I've never seen it like this."

"Smile."

I turned around and saw that he had his phone in his hand.

"I'll take a picture and send it to you," he said. "So you can see what I see."

I pushed my hair back and smiled.

Then he lowered his phone, and I heard mine ping a second later.

"Thanks," I said, grateful that he'd thought to capture what was such a personal moment for me.

His dark eyes smiled before he looked past me again. "I want the inside of the place to match the way it looks from here," he said. "That's my goal, in case you were wondering."

"I'd like that, too."

"Do you mind if we take one together?" he asked, raising his eyebrows.

"Not at all," I said, scooting over.

He squeezed onto the bench beside me and raised his phone in front of us.

I smiled and cocked my head towards his.

"Thanks," he said, his hand touching my knee as he headed back to his seat.

My whole thigh felt like it had gone up in flames, and I wondered if he still wanted me the way he did before or if he'd tired of my bad attitude and decided I was more trouble than I was worth.

Then again, he did get carrot cake.

We got stuck into the picnic and talked until the sun moved around the edge of the world, going through enough wine that I felt compelled to close my eyes occasionally and focus on the boat's gentle rocking.

By the time we turned back, half the sky was lit up with stars like a navy blanket decorated with delicate gold thread while the other half still glowed the same faint yellow that one might expect from a sleepy firefly.

I enjoyed the cool evening breeze as I relaxed on a cushioned bench behind Adam, watching as he steered the boat back to the marina, his shoulders as broad as the shiny wooden wheel.

I offered to help when we entered the port, but he told me to stay where I was so I watched him move deliberately around the dock like a capable member of Jack Sparrow's crew- except for the fact that he was way better looking.

"We've arrived safely at our destination m'lady," he said after securing the ropes to the dock and joining me at the back of the boat.

I glanced at my nearly empty glass and stood up. "You never made your toast."

He grabbed the wine and poured a sip in his empty glass, his chiseled face lit up by the bright evening sky.

"Well?" I asked.

"To our second date," he said, lifting his drink. "May it be even more enjoyable."

The part of me that hesitated didn't react fast enough to stop me from clinking my glass against his before downing my last sip.

"I had a really good time tonight," he said, stepping up to me.

"Me too," I said, staying where I was.

Adam lifted his hand and tilted my chin up gently.

I lost myself in his dark eyes, forgetting all the reasons I couldn't have him. Then I let him kiss me, and I kissed him back, savoring the way his lips felt against mine before his tongue twirled in my mouth, igniting a fire in my core that made me crave every inch of him.

When he sealed my lips with a kiss and pulled back, he rested his head against my forehead. "I've got bad news," he whispered.

I laid a hand on his chest and looked up at him, my eyes searching his. "What is it?"

"That didn't break the spell," he said, brushing the back of his fingertips against my cheek.

"Can I be honest with you?"

He nodded.

I pressed my lips together and smiled. "I was hoping it wouldn't."

FLASHBACK
- Adam-

"I can't believe you get to live here year round," I said, handing the rum to Jolie.

"It is pretty sweet," she said, taking a swig.

I watched her exhale sharply as the cheap liquor burned its way down her throat.

"Did you leave your shoes by the campfire, too?" I asked, noticing we were both barefoot in the dark sand.

She dropped her arm so the bottle swung at her side and looked back. The fire was still glowing in the distance, a dozen dark silhouettes moving around it. Their muffled debauchery was barely audible over the crashing waves. "I guess I did."

"Do you want to go back?"

She waved the suggestion away. "No. They're not going to walk away without my feet in them."

"True."

She handed the bottle back to me.

"You want to sit down?" I asked, her sparkly belly button ring catching my eye.

"Up a little further," she said. "There's a good spot."

I wanted to ask where exactly, but I didn't want to blow my chances with her by asking too many questions. She was the coolest girl I'd ever met, and everything she did seemed to be intoxicating me further.

Not once had she complained that I didn't have a chaser for the rum, and the way she'd poked fun at Christophe for trying so hard to impress Gia made me laugh so much I could still feel the stitches in my side.

"There," she said, trudging through the soft sand towards the dunes.

I followed her, my eyes dropping to the barely there jean shorts that covered her ass as she ducked between a gap in the dunes.

For a moment, I feared my eyes were playing tricks on me and that I'd imagined her like a shipwrecked sailor imagines a mermaid. But after a few steps, I found her again in a small dip in the sand that was surrounded by tall sea oats.

"Quite the hideaway," I said, taking another swig as I joined her, feeling encouraged that she'd led me somewhere we could be alone.

"I want to show you something," she said.

Every cell in my body perked up.

She collapsed in the sand and leaned back. "Lay down."

I laid next to her and looked up at the sky. "What are we-"

"Shhh," she said. "Listen to the sea oats."

I stared at the starry sky and listened as the breeze rustled the sea oats around us. It was so loud I was surprised I hadn't noticed it before, and the rustling came in waves of intensity, just like the ocean crashing against the shore.

I opened my mouth to make fun of her for being drunk, but the more I listened, the more overwhelming the sound became. It was beautiful and worthwhile and nothing short of an orchestra. I'd never heard anything like it.

"What do you think?" she finally whispered.

"I'm blown away," I said, rolling my head towards her.

She smiled and sat up. "It's one of my favorite songs."

"Do you have a name for it?" I asked, propping myself up on my elbows. It was darker in the pit than it had been on the moonlit beach, and if it weren't for the starry sky, I wouldn't have been able to make out the delicate features of her face.

She shook her head. "No. Some things are too pretty to have a name."

I wanted to say something clever about her name meaning pretty in French, but my romantic intentions were no match for my tipsiness.

"You know what else I like about this spot?" she asked, pulling her shirt off to reveal a white string bikini.

I swallowed.

"No one will steal our rum while we're swimming."

I raised my eyebrows. "You want to go for a swim?"

229

She shrugged. "Why not?"

"I don't have my bathing suit."

Her lips curled into a smile. "I guess you'll have to skinny dip."

"I will if you will," I said, pulling my sandy t-shirt off.

She looked down, her eyelashes casting shadows on her cheeks.

I unzipped my shorts and wiggled out of them so I was sitting in the sand in my boxers.

Her eyes traveled up my chest. Then she reached for the rum and took a swig.

"What are you thinking?" I asked.

She unzipped her shorts and wriggled out of them so she was sitting in the sand, her glowing bikini calling my attention to her most intriguing parts. "I'm thinking about whether I want to let you see me naked."

I scooted into her personal space.

She stopped breathing as I reached around her back to where her bikini was tied.

I kept my eyes on hers as I pulled the string and leaned forward to kiss her. She tasted like spiced rum, and when the strings fell loose around my wrist, I moved my hand to her breast, letting her puckered nipple graze my palm as I laid her back in the sand.

The sound of her breathing mingled with the fluttering sea oats as I kissed my way down her delicate tan lines, stopping at her chest to take one of her nipples in my mouth.

"Adam," she whispered.

I raised up on an elbow and looked down to admire the way her hair was splayed in the sand behind her head. "What?" I asked, sliding my hand down her stomach and into her bikini bottom.

Her parted lips were motionless as I dragged my fingers along her wet slit.

She reached down and pulled the strings on one side of her hips loose, and when her eyelids grew heavy, I spread her warm silk around her clit and pushed my fingers inside her.

Her breath hitched in her throat as she arched her back, and she stared at me through glassy eyes as I curled my fingers inside her. Then she reached up and pulled my face down so she could kiss me deeply again as I fingered her.

A moment later, she moaned in my mouth, and I got so hard my whole body ached.

I slipped my dripping fingers from her and pulled the ties on the other side of her suit. Then, without pulling my mouth from hers, I pushed my boxers down over my hips.

I had no choice but to pull back for a second as I forced them down my legs.

When I looked back at her, she was staring at my dick with a look of curious innocence on her face that made me want her more than I ever thought I'd want anyone.

"I'm a virgin," she said, her eyes searching mine.

"It's okay," I whispered, dragging a thumb over her cheek.

"Do you know what you're doing?"

I nodded. It wasn't a complete lie. After all, I knew exactly how sex was supposed to work. I just hadn't actually had it myself yet.

She ran a hand down my chest and bit her lip. "Okay."

I kissed her again and shifted my body over her as I reached for my dick. Then I guided it inside her as slow as my eager hips would allow, conscious of the way she gripped my shoulders like it would all be okay if she just held on.

She was so tight I couldn't keep my eyes open, and her moans were so soft I could only hear them in the breaks between the crashing waves, but I took it as slow as I could, my hips swaying with the sea oats as I buried myself in the most beautiful girl I'd ever known.

Naturally, the feeling of being clenched inside her warmth was better than I ever imagined it could be, but it was a different feeling that would move to the front of my mind as the years went on, a different feeling that I became obsessed with having again.

And that feeling was the way she held on to me as I moved over her, the way her hands held me so tight I thought she'd never let go, the way it felt to have her trust and her body at the same time.

It was a high I never found again.

And while we never did go skinny dipping that night, I wouldn't have changed a thing.

TWENTY FOUR
- Adam -

I would normally send a woman flowers after a date, but flowers seemed like too much and too little at the same time.

Too much because I was aware that she didn't want to attract attention to our extracurricular relationship. Plus, getting her to agree to a second date was a big enough victory that I didn't want to risk blowing it with unwelcome romantic gestures.

Too little because it's what I would do for any woman, and she meant so much more to me than the other women I'd sent flowers to. She deserved something as unique as she was.

To say I was overjoyed when I thought of the perfect thing would be an understatement, and I'd just chosen the words for the gift card and clicked overnight delivery when I heard a knock on the door.

"Come in," I said, closing the tab on my laptop as soon as I saw the confirmation that my order was complete.

"Hello," Gia said, ducking her head in. "Are you ready for me?"

I glanced between the clock and the spreadsheet on my desk. "Of course. Please have a seat."

She teetered in on high heels, clutching a manila folder to her chest.

"Thanks so much for coming," I said. "I've been looking forward to seeing what you've come up with."

She smiled and sat down, scooting a chair right up to the opposite side of my desk. "When you first mentioned the assignment, I was worried that I didn't have any other interests," she said. "But once I started looking, it was hard to narrow down all the things I got excited about."

"That's great," I said, folding my hands in front of me. "That's the whole point of this exercise."

She batted her dark lashes.

"I know there are a lot of ways to run a business, but I don't want to be one of those bosses that's so naïve as to reduce the people I work with to whatever their main job description is. I've found that the more you encourage people to grow and the more challenged they feel at work, the happier they are."

"Well," she said, shifting in her seat to cross her legs. "Everyone who's met with you so far has been really excited so you must be doing something right."

I nodded. "Good. Let's get started then shall we?"

"Okay."

"First- just so I understand your main responsibilities at the minute," I said, flipping through a binder on my desk. "Your regular duties include managing reception, concierge services, taking orders for room service, and assisting in the interview process for the housekeeping department. Correct?"

"Yes," she said. "And I don't want you to think I don't love those things when I show you how far out the other jobs I liked are."

"Not to worry," I said. "Lay it on me."

"I like to work out," she said, opening her folder and laying out a job post she printed off the internet. "I always thought I'd make a good fitness instructor."

"Are you familiar with water aerobics?" I asked.

She shook her head. "Just regular aerobics. Why?"

"That's a service I'd like to start offering a few days a week," I said. "In the mornings during high season. I've been asking around and several of the female guests I've surveyed have said that's something they would take advantage of."

She raised her eyebrows.

"Is that something you might be interested in organizing and leading?" I asked.

"Sure," she said. "That could be fun. Plus, it would free up time outside work that I usually have to spend at the gym."

"Great. Let's give it a try. Figure out what kind of schedule you think would make sense, and we'll offer it for a limited time to see if it catches on."

"Who would work reception if I did that?"

I smiled, pleased that her regular duties were still at the front of her mind. "There are two girls working in the restaurant who are hospitality majors, and they've both expressed interest in gaining some new skills to put on their resumes. I'm sure they could cover for you."

"Cool."

"What's next?" I asked, nodding towards the folder.

Her other interests included bartending and being a game show host, though she hadn't found any job postings for the latter. I said I'd talk to the head barman about her learning a few drinks.

Unfortunately, I couldn't wave a magic wand and make her the host of her own TV show, but as a consolation prize, I asked if she'd be interested in planning and publicizing a sand castle competition for Fourth of July weekend.

At first she seemed skeptical, but when I told her she'd get a commission on every participant she enrolled, she perked right up and started selling me the idea as if it had been her own.

She was so convincing I was tempted to tell her I also wanted to run beach Olympics for the crowd that came in August before school started. But I decided to save the idea for a rainy day and see how the sand castle challenge went first.

Much to my disappointment, Gia didn't spill anything about Jolie during our conversation, and I didn't know whether to be discouraged or encouraged by that.

After all, I was under the impression that she told Gia everything. Then again, I hadn't blabbed about our night out to anyone either so maybe she was just trying to get her head around the untimely but unusual connection we had.

We were wrapping things up when my phone buzzed against the desk for the third time in a row. "Sorry," I said. "I better get that."

"Sure thing," she said, closing her folder and standing up.

"Hi," I said, taking the call. "Can you hold on a second?"

Gia was backing out with a raised palm in the air.

"Great meeting with you," I said. "Let me know by the end of the week how soon you think we can roll out the water aerobics."

She nodded and let herself out.

I took a deep breath and lifted the phone to my ear. "Victoria, hi."

"Hi."

"Is everything okay?" I asked.

"I was calling to ask you the same question," she said, her tone of voice prim and tight.

"Everything's great," I said. "Why?"

"You missed my sister's twenty ninth birthday."

I squinted. "You mean her thirty third birthday?"

"Don't be a jerk."

"I wasn't," I said. "Just wanted to make sure I had the right sister."

"You were supposed to be there," she said. "You promised you would make it."

I pinched the bridge of my nose. "I know I did, Vic, but I made that promise back when we were together and before I knew I'd be down here for the summer."

"That's no excuse."

I furrowed my brow. "I think it is. I'm not your boyfriend anymore. That means I'm no longer obligated to accompany you to your tri monthly family functions."

"Everyone was asking about you."

I leaned back in my chair. "That's nice."

"Not for me it wasn't," she said. "I organized the whole thing and then showed up alone."

"You didn't even remind me about it. Surely you knew I wasn't coming."

"I was testing you," she hissed. "And you failed."

"That's insane. I was very clear last time we spoke that we're no longer an item."

"You didn't make it clear to your mother."

"Excuse me?" I asked.

"She and I were at lunch the other day when I realized you hadn't even told her that you tried to break up with me."

"First of all, I'm not sure what the word 'tried' was doing in that sentence. Second of all, why the hell were you having lunch with my mother?"

Victoria let out a heavy sigh. "Because we have a relationship, Adam, and when I have a relationship with someone, I take it seriously."

I dropped my head back.

"Don't worry," she said. "I didn't tell her about all the unkind things you said."

I shook my head. "What unkind things? That I didn't want to see you anymore and that I thought you'd be happier with someone else?"

"Enough. I didn't call to rehash all those painful comments."

I craned my neck forward. "Why did you call exactly?"

"To let you know that you needn't worry about her, that I'm looking after her, and that I didn't tell her about the momentary lapse in judgement you experienced before you left."

I scratched my head.

"And also," she continued. "I forgive you."

I suppressed my urge to laugh out loud. "Victoria."

"Yes."

"I need you to listen very carefully."

"Listening."

"You and I are not dating anymore, which means the last place you should expect to bump into me is at one of your family parties."

"But-"

"And I didn't realize it before, but obviously I need to spell out the fact that if we're not seeing each other anymore, you shouldn't be seeing my mother either."

"We have a special bond, Adam."

"I don't know who you're referring to now, but I don't care. You need to move on."

"Put Adam back on the phone. This is obviously not the man I fell in love with."

"Cut the crap, Vic. It's over. Leave me and my family alone, and find someone else to mother."

And with that, I hung up the phone and blocked her number.

TWENTY FIVE
- Jolie -

Adam wasn't the only one under a spell. Ever since our date, I'd been a distracted mess.

I was putting away dishes in the fridge and leaving milk in the cupboard. I was humming to myself and smiling for no reason. I'd even caught myself doodling his name again like a love-struck teenager.

It was a feeling I knew all too well, a feeling I'd had before.

And I swear I was as excited about that slow burning kiss he gave me on the boat as I had been that night I let him take my virginity in the sand with only a sliver of moon to keep us company.

It hurt a little that first time, but not in a bad way. Whatever pain I felt was overwhelmed by the fact that I'd never felt closer to anyone, safer with anyone, more attracted to anyone.

And he was so gentle with me, which was more than I could say for the boys I'd fooled around with before he came along. They were clumsy and hurried and obviously only thinking about themselves.

But Adam hadn't been like that. Not once had he made me feel faceless or used or like a means to an end. On the contrary, it was all about me, and that made the feelings I had for him penetrate far deeper than even his physical reach allowed.

I became a woman that night under the stars, and I knew it wasn't a dream because I was sore in an awkward way that made me giddy for days afterwards.

Still, we managed to find our way back there the very next night. And the next and the next. And when we couldn't make it as far as the secret dune, we fucked in my car after dark or the locker room after hours. We even did it in his hotel room a few times when his parents went golfing.

And it wasn't just the sex I fell in love with. It was the way he looked at me before and after, his eyes drinking me in like I was a unicorn shrouded in mist.

He was the only boy that ever made me feel that way, like my quirks and body were unique. Even I looked at my body differently after that summer, and I had him to thank for that.

It was as if his attention woke me up to my own strength.

But he was a man now, a man that would probably do a whole lot more than kiss me if I let him.

And as opposed to the idea as I'd been before our date, something in me had shifted while we were out on the water.

Maybe it was thinking about my dad and realizing how fleeting life could be. Or perhaps it was realizing that Adam was one of the good guys and that I'd be a fool to turn away the affection he wanted to show me.

Whatever it was, my interest in getting to know him better was now outshining my desire to keep him at a distance, and the only issue I had with that development was the fact that I couldn't wipe the goddamn smile off my face.

What's more, the good feelings swirling inside me, which had been awakened by a mere kiss as if I were living in a fucking fairy tale, were affecting more than just my relations with my employer.

They were softening me, softening me so much I decided to start having coffee in the mornings with my mom again.

"So how's it going?" she asked, as if I hadn't been avoiding her for weeks.

"How's what going?"

She made her way over with our favorite mugs. "Work."

"Good," I said, laying out two reed coasters. "We've been implementing some exciting changes that I think will have a positive impact on the hotel's earning potential going forward."

"That's nice to hear," she said, sitting in the chair across the table.

"The new furniture in the lobby looks fantastic for one thing," I said. "It's made the hotel feel really fresh and welcoming."

She nodded.

"And we've been adding new activities for the guests to enjoy."

"Oh?" She raised her eyebrows. "Like what?"

"Like Gia's started teaching water aerobics three mornings a week, and it's had an instant effect on the vibe at the pool since the mothers are getting to know each other better."

"Wow."

"And we're going to have a sand castle contest on Fourth of July weekend followed by a barbeque so people will stay and spend money when the contest is over."

"That sounds wonderful."

I nodded and slid my mug towards me.

"And what about Adam?" she asked.

I swallowed.

"Has the staff warmed to him okay?"

"Yeah, he's great," I said as casually as I could. "Best of all, he's convinced everyone to take on more responsibility while somehow convincing them that it was their idea."

She squinted.

"It's complicated," I said. "But trust me. Whatever he's doing is working and the staff seem happier than ever."

She pressed her thin lips together and blinked. "Does this mean you forgive me?"

"There's nothing to forgive."

She cocked her head. "That's not true, honey. You were right to be upset, and I've been dealing with a lot of guilt over the decision I made to sell the place."

I looked at her bare face. It seemed to be aging so much faster since my dad's passing. "You don't need to feel guilty, Mom."

"I can't help it."

I reached forward and put a hand over hers. "I understand why you made the choice that you did, and the hotel is going to be better for it."

Her eyes searched mine. "You really think so?"

"I know so," I said, squeezing her hand. "And that's all that really matters." I pulled my hand back and wrapped it around my mug. "I thought you were giving up on the hotel when you sold it, but I realize now that you were doing what you had to in order to save it."

Her eyes watered. "Thanks, Jolie. It means a lot to me that you understand."

"Of course."

She took a deep breath.

"Sorry I can't stay," I said. "I have to cover for Gia during her class."

"Before you go-" She pushed herself back from the table and stood up. "A package came for you this morning."

"A package?" I furrowed my brow and downed the rest of my coffee.

She walked to the front of the house and returned a moment later with what looked like an extra long shoe box. "You didn't order this?"

I shook my head as I took it from her, but deep down in my guts, I knew there was only one person it could be from. "Thanks," I said, opening the door.

"You're not going to open it now?" she asked, her disappointment obvious.

"I can't," I lied. "I'll be late." I gave her a kiss on the cheek and hurried to my car where it was parked in the street. As soon as I sat inside, I sliced the brown tape with my car key and slid the box open.

There was a colorful kite inside, and according to the picture on the outside of the clear package, it would look like a giant seahorse when it was flying.

When I freed it from the box, a small envelope fell onto my lap. I laid the kite on the passenger seat and turned my attention to the note.

Inside, a card held a message printed in a mysterious little font.

Here's a clue

For date number two

If you can't find me in the dunes,

Use the kite & I'll find you xx

TWENTY SIX
- Adam -

I was sitting on a blanket in the dugout dune looking for a flying seahorse when Jolie appeared in the path between the sea oats.

"Well, well, well," she said, cocking her hip. "What do we have here?"

"You found me," I said, sitting up.

She was in a little black sundress that had a gold zipper running all the way up to a hint of cleavage.

"I was starting to lose hope."

"I can't believe you found this place again," she said, dropping to her knees at the edge of the blanket and setting the kite down beside her.

"Of course I did," I said, moving the small cooler and takeout bag so she'd have more room.

"Another picnic?" she asked, kicking her legs out to the side.

"Is that okay with you?" I asked, unzipping the fabric cooler and pulling out two beers. "I get kind of sick of fancy restaurants."

She raised her eyebrows.

"Okay," I said, popping the caps off the beers. "I realize how that sounded."

"It's fine," she said. "I like picnics."

I passed her a bottle.

"Thanks," she said, clinking it against mine.

"The menu's not as varied as last time," I said, passing the paper bag over to her as I took a sip of beer.

She opened it and looked inside, her face lighting up when she saw the familiar cardboard containers. "You got Nino's calzones?"

"I hope that's cool. I know you eat them all the time, but-"

"It's more than cool," she said, removing one of the boxes. "It's a wonderful surprise."

"I haven't actually had one yet."

She furrowed her brow. "What the heck have you been eating? This is the best takeout within a hundred miles of here."

I shrugged. "I think I've had the Harmony Bay Club Sandwich seven hundred times."

She laughed.

"To be honest, though, I was hoping the calzone wouldn't be my only first of the night."

"What do you mean?" she asked, pulling some plastic cutlery out of the bag and handing me a fork and knife.

I pulled a small lantern from the cooler and lit the candle inside it.

"Fancy," she said, cutting the corner off her calzone.

"I try," I said, setting it beside us. It was a bit early for candlelight, but the sky over the ocean was already getting darker, and the soft yellow glow overhead would be gone within the hour.

"So what other first did you have in mind?" she asked, her eyes flashing up at me as she took another bite.

"Remember the first time we were here?"

She pulled her long hair in front of one shoulder. "I do."

I broke the corner off my calzone. "Remember how we were going to go skinny dipping?"

She licked her lips. "I remember what we did instead."

"Well, I've still never done that."

She squinted at me. "What do you mean you've never done that?"

"I've never been skinny dipping."

She took a sip of beer. "How is that even possible?"

"It just hasn't happened," I said, letting my eyes follow the thin straps of her sandals from her ankle to where they were tied halfway up her tanned shins. "I almost did once."

"What happened?"

"I was on a Grecian Island with some friends-"

She nodded as she chewed.

"And right when I was stripped down with one foot in the water, one of my friends started screaming like a banshee."

She covered her full mouth. "Why?"

"He stepped on a sea urchin."

She scrunched her face. "Oh dear."

"Needless to say, I did a one eighty."

"Understandable."

"So what do you think?" I asked, popping some calzone in my mouth.

"I'm not sure," she said. "To be honest, I'm a little confused."

"Why?"

"I thought we were starting over, but it kind of sounds like you want to relive some childhood fantasy."

"It's more like I consider skinny dipping a bucket list item, and since it's unfinished business that I had with you, I thought we might finish what we started."

Her eyes flashed up at me. "I think you're just trying to get me naked."

My mouth curled into a smile. "Is it that obvious?"

"Yeah."

"Nothing I haven't seen before."

"And what if I say yes?" she asked. "What if I say yes and you're disappointed because nothing is how you remembered it?"

"Is that a joke?"

"No. It's a serious question."

"Have you gotten something pierced that you want to tell me about?" I asked.

"No, but I did get a tattoo a few years ago."

"Of what?" I asked.

"You don't know?"

I shook my head. "How could I?"

"You really have no idea?"

"Should I know?" I asked. "Is it something obvious?"

She cocked her head.

"Like a paddle board or the sun or a dolphin or some shit?"

"No," she said, fixing her eyes on mine. "It's a seahorse."

"You're joking."

She shook her head.

"That's a coincidence."

"You're sure you didn't see it that night after the party when I had my shirt off and-"

"Should I have? Where is it?"

"I don't know if I should kill you or believe you."

"Maybe you should show it to me," I said. "I'm sure I'll recognize it if I've seen it before."

She laughed. "Like a police lineup? Like 'Do you recognize any of these seahorses, sir?'"

"I'm seriously replaying that night in my mind over and over, but-"

"Well stop doing that," she said.

"So where is it?"

She cocked an arm and pressed a finger just below the outside edge of her left breast.

"How would I have seen it? You had a bra on."

"So you say," she said. "But you could've peeked."

"Please tell me you don't really think I would do that."

"I don't," she said. "But the kite-"

"Was just a coincidence."

"In that case," she said, slicing through another cheesy bite of calzone. "It was very thoughtful, and I appreciate it."

"You're welcome. I thought you would prefer it to flowers."

"You were going to get me flowers?"

"Of course," I said. "That boat ride was the most fun I've had with a woman since I was seventeen."

She blushed. "I had fun, too."

"Good. Because I really like you, Jolie. I've liked you since the day I met you, and I know I'm supposed to stop because we work together, but I can't."

She pursed her lips and set her fork down. "I don't want you to stop. I really like you, too."

I slid her takeout container out of the way so I could scoot closer. "Even when I'm obviously trying to trick you into getting naked?"

"Oh my god you're still thinking about my tattoo."

"I think I'm going to go crazy if you don't show it to me."

She twisted her mouth like she was considering it. "I don't show it to very many people."

I grew hard at the thought of seeing it up close.

She batted her heavy lashes. "It's kind of a shy seahorse."

TWENTY SEVEN
- Jolie -

It was all so surreal and romantic, and being back in that hidden dune with him was making me feel young again.

Here was this amazing guy who was as thoughtful as he was successful and handsome, and he was acting like there was nothing he wanted more in the whole world than to see my silly little tattoo.

What's more, he'd bought me a kite of my favorite animal on a whim before surprising me with beer and my favorite takeout in what was hands down my favorite place on Earth.

I stared into his dark eyes and listened to the sea oats rustling in the breeze.

Part of me felt like it was a trap. It was too full on- the seduction, the look in his eyes, the coincidences. It all seemed too good to be true.

But at the same time, I couldn't shake the feeling that I should let myself be swept up in it.

Why shouldn't a great guy be interested in me? Why shouldn't a great guy spoil me a little?

Just because I'd never known the kind of gut churning feeling I felt with him didn't mean I should run away. Not that I could possibly run. I felt too much like I was leaning into the wind over a great cliff, my arms spread as if I were flying.

And the darker it got, the more familiar it all felt.

I wasn't nearly as hammered as I'd been on that first rum filled night we spent together, of course. But I had a solid buzz going and Adam was making me laugh with such frequency it was as if he'd deactivated every line of defense I had.

"I've been thinking about that kiss," he said. "The one on the boat."

I turned my gaze from the starry sky and looked at him.

"It's been driving me to distraction."

"Really?" I asked, crossing my ankles.

"I tried to get in the wrong car in the parking lot twice," he said. "And I got lost on one of my morning runs this past week."

"You got lost?"

He nodded. "I was just running along- thinking about kissing you- and then bam, I was in Leopardstown."

I craned my neck forward. "Are you kidding? That's so far away!"

"I realize that," he said. "Halfway back I hailed a taxi."

I laughed. "Anything else?"

"I forgot to eat lunch on Wednesday."

"Shit, Adam. I'm sorry."

"Don't be. It was the best week I've had in ages."

"Maybe it's best that I don't kiss you again," I said, suppressing a smile. "I'd hate to make things worse for you."

"I was thinking the opposite," he said. "I'm convinced the only way to find peace again would be to kiss you a thousand times."

"A thousand times?!"

"Or as many times as it takes for it to not feel like such a big deal anymore."

I glanced at his lips.

"Which might only be twice. It's hard to say."

"Twice?!" I smacked him in the arm.

"All I need is your permission," he said. "And I'll leave no stone unturned."

"What does that mean?"

"It means I'm going to kiss every inch of you until I find that damn seahorse, and I'm not going to stop there."

The thought of him kissing me naked in the sand again was enough to make me wet.

"But there's something I have to tell you first."

"What?" I asked, my stomach tightening.

"I haven't been completely honest with you."

I knew it. I knew it. I knew it. None of this is real. What was I thinking?

"I lied to you," he said. "A long time ago."

I furrowed my brow. "What are you talking about?"

"It only seemed like a white lie at the time."

"You're freaking me out, Adam."

"I was just trying to do the right thing."

"Spit it out already."

"Do you remember the first night we came here?" he asked.

I nodded as blurry memories flashed through my mind.

"Remember when you told me you were a virgin?" he asked. "And you asked me if I knew what I was doing?"

I swallowed. "Yes."

"Well, I didn't."

"What are you saying?"

"I was a virgin, too."

My eyes grew wide.

He looked back at me, his gaze so unflinching I knew in my heart he was telling the truth.

"I was your first?" I asked.

He nodded.

"I don't understand," I said. "Why would you lie about that?"

He shrugged. "I've wondered that myself over the years."

"And have you drawn any conclusions?"

"I think I wanted you to feel like you were in safe hands."

"I did," I said. *I still do.*

"I'm sorry I lied to you."

"It's okay," I said. "I don't wish things happened any differently."

"I won't ever lie to you again."

I sat up and turned towards him. "Why are you telling me this now?"

"Because I need you to believe me when I say I've been crazy about you since that night." He clenched his jaw. "To be fair, I think I was crazy about you before then, but I didn't know how deep my feelings went."

"And now you do?"

He bowed his head.

"How deep?" I asked, my chest fluttering.

"I can't tell you in words."

"Then show me," I said, laying a hand on his chest and clenching the fabric of his collared shirt in my fist.

He leaned forward and kissed me then until my whole body boiled inside.

His kisses were urgent, deep, hungry, and just when I'd run out of breath, he pulled back. "I'm not going to be able to stop once I start touching you," he said, his fingers finding the zipper at the top of my cleavage. "If you aren't going to let me have all of you, you have to say so right now."

"I won't stop you," I said, my breath mingling with his. "You can have all of me." *You've always had me anyway.*

He began sliding the zipper down past my breasts at a speed that was as deliberate as it was intense.

And when the zipper reached the bottom, my dress fell open so the cool evening breeze awakened my skin.

"I assume you've learned a few things since the last time we did this," I said, sliding my hand around the back of his neck.

"You tell me," he said.

And with that, he lowered me down on my back and made a woman of me all over again.

TWENTY EIGHT
- Adam -

The taste of her salty tongue intensified the scent of the soft sea breeze, and as the sky darkened above us, my desire for her overwhelmed me.

I dropped my lips to her neck and pressed my fingers between her legs so I could feel the heat through her black lace panties.

Despite how much I ached for her, I wanted to make the moment last. I pulled my hand back and slid it up her stomach to her chest, where the peaks of her perfect breasts were suspended in a black bra that looked delicate enough to eat.

"Getting warmer," she said, arching her back.

I assumed she was talking about her tattoo and reached around to unhook her bra. As soon as it came loose, I pushed it up her chest to release her breasts and lowered my mouth to her nipples, which rose to attention when I twirled my tongue around them.

Her skin was sweet and smelled of an intoxicating citrus perfume. I kissed the soft curve below her right breast before moving towards the other one.

"Well?" she asked.

I lifted my face to look into her dark eyes.

"You sure you haven't seen that before?"

Oh right- the tattoo. I glanced back down to where the curve of her left breast met her side and narrowed my lust blurred gaze in an attempt to focus on the image.

It was smaller than my thumb, but thanks to the bright colors and the candlelight flickering against her skin, I could make out the intricate design.

"What do you think?" she asked.

"I think it makes your tits look huge."

She rolled her eyes and pushed my chest away, but I was kissing her again a moment later, massaging her breasts in my hand as I swelled for her.

"Take this off," I breathed against her, pulling her up so she could get her arms out of the sleeves of her dress. Once that was done, she pulled her bra off and tossed it to the side.

The sight of her tanned body spread out on the blanket made my mouth water, inciting a thirst that could only be clenched in one way.

I leaned up and pulled my own shirt off before scooting down so I could pull off her panties.

She leaned her head up and watched me, her chest rising and falling with her breath.

When I saw her pussy I felt like I might cry. It was perfectly groomed, and the sight of a familiar beauty mark brought back memories I'd forgotten about.

"Adam," she said, reading my expression. "You don't have to-"

"Oh but I do," I said, pushing her legs apart and lowering myself between them.

When my tongue first touched her, she let out the lightest sigh, and it wasn't long before she was dripping wet.

I lapped at her slit with an enthusiasm I didn't know I had in me.

"Oh god," she whispered as I picked up the pace, flicking her swollen bud with my tongue and scooping her out so I wouldn't miss a drop. "You're going to make me come."

I thought about stopping, but she was too delicious, and the sexy sound of her panting spurred me on.

Once she'd jerked a few times, I knew she was on the brink, and I wanted to quench my thirst with her pleasure.

I stuck my fingers inside her, and she groaned as I churned her desire until it dripped across my palm.

I didn't know a woman could be so wet, so delicious, and I curled my fingers inside her as I lapped at her clit, my lips slippery with her silk.

"I'm coming," she whispered, sinking her fingers into the blanket beneath her.

A moment later, her body jerked so hard she nearly sat up, and I pulled my fingers out so her orgasm could flow down my throat, the taste of her bliss filling me up.

She spasmed when I tried to touch her clit after that, as if my fingers were electrified.

When her breathing slowed, I dragged my mouth against her inner thigh and propped myself up.

She looked as if she could barely keep her eyes open. "That was incredible."

I raised up on my knees and unzipped my navy shorts.

Her eyes dripped down my chest to the trail of hair above my waistband.

I pulled my shorts off with my boxers, admiring the way the candlelight flickered against her soft curves. I was about to lower myself over her when she sat up, and I felt my swollen cock surge under the gaze of her attention.

She reached for it and stroked me until my whole face twisted.

"Fuck," I breathed, her taste on my lips as I watched her.

By the time she leaned forward and licked my head, it was all I could do not to collapse.

Finally, she twirled her tongue around my sensitive tip, flashed her big brown eyes at me, and sank me against the back of her throat.

After two bobs of her head, I needed something to hold on to, so I rested a palm against her soft hair and let my head fall back as she sucked me.

"Fuck," I mouthed, but no sound came out as I lost myself under the spell of her touch.

I couldn't believe it. Even in my wildest dreams I never expected her to devour me like that. And the surprise of it caught me so off guard I could've sworn I felt feelings for her bubble up inside me that I wasn't ready to have.

When her free hand cupped my balls, I clenched a bunch of her hair in my fist and struggled to keep my hips from moving.

But as much as I wanted to watch her milk my dick, I needed to be inside her, needed to feel her body clench around me like it had all those years ago.

"Jolie," I whispered. "Jolie stop."

She slid her warm mouth off my dick and looked up at me, her eyes dark and shiny.

"I need to be inside you."

She leaned back on the blanket again and propped herself up on her elbows.

My eyes ran up her center and stopped on her lips.

When she licked them, it felt like she was daring me and inviting me at the same time.

I lowered myself over her, the cool breeze on my ass a million miles away from the heat I could feel rising up between her legs. I took my dick in my hands and guided it to her opening, keeping my eyes on hers as I pushed my way in.

"Oh god," she said, dropping to her back beneath me. "You feel even bigger than I remember."

I slid a hand behind her neck and dragged my thumb across her throat. "And you feel just as tight," I breathed, sinking all the way inside her.

Then I lowered my lips and pressed them to hers, kissing her deeply as I rocked my hips over her and relished the way her soaked pussy gushed around me.

She slid her fingers into my hair as I massaged her insides with my every swollen inch. And as I picked up the pace, her hands dropped to my back, her nails digging into me as I drove inside her.

She let out a wild groan and dropped her head back, tilting her hips against the blanket so I could hit her deeper. "Don't stop," she begged. "Right there."

I stared at her lips and came then, shaking over her as I pumped her full of everything I had. Then I collapsed on top of her so heavily I could feel our hearts beating against each other.

"Your skills have come a long way," she whispered against my neck as I throbbed inside her.

"I was hoping you'd say that," I said, lifting my face to look at her.

And when her eyes smiled at me, I knew it was love.

TWENTY NINE
- Jolie -

It was late by the time we headed back to the hotel, but it was the most glorious walk of my life.

Adam somehow managed to carry everything along with holding my hand, which was good because otherwise I might have floated away like a balloon.

I felt both carefree and exhausted in the best way, and I was grateful for the loudness of the crashing waves as it distracted me from trying to label my feelings further.

But there was one thing I did know, and that was that I didn't want the high to end.

Fortunately, my mind was too busy setting off fireworks for me to dwell on the consequences of my newfound smitteness. I mean, how was I going to be professional at work now that I'd given my boss head on the beach?!

Of course, I was so far gone I didn't care how it sounded. Nor did I care that my black underwear was drenched or that I'd looked him in the eye and let him see how much I wanted him back.

Yes, my cover was well and truly blown, but so was his. And I don't know if I was too physically worn out to be anxious of if I was genuinely confident in the fact that we could figure things out together, but I was more calm and at peace than I'd been in years.

In fact, my guard was so far down, I walked right up to the hotel without thinking of letting go of his hand… Until he let go of mine in the lobby so abruptly it was almost as if he'd shoved it away.

"Adam. I was beginning to worry that your father was wrong about you staying here."

I turned towards the voice to find an elderly woman sitting on the new couch. She seemed physically weak despite the fact that her face looked eerily young, as if she'd had lots of work done on it.

Beside her, a porcelain skinned woman with deep red lips and shiny black hair was perched on the edge of her cushion, an expensive handbag resting on her lap like a cat.

"Mom," Adam said, freezing where he stood.

I narrowed my eyes at her, and as they adjusted to the lights in the lobby, I realized that I did faintly recognize the woman. The younger lady, however, was definitely a new face, and she had that entitled look about her, like she couldn't have lowered her nose if she wanted to.

Adam headed over to his mom.

She rose to her feet to greet him. "You forgot our anniversary, honey," his mom said as she reached up to hug him.

"What are you doing here?" he asked.

She raised her painted eyebrows. "When Victoria said she couldn't get you on the phone, I got very worried."

"I'm fine," he said. "You shouldn't have traveled."

I looked over my shoulder. One of the summer staff was standing behind the reception desk listening to headphones and swiping at her phone. Despite how horrified I was, I was relieved to see she was distracted.

"Excuse me." His mother waved a finger at me. "Maybe you could arrange to have someone take our bags."

My lips fell apart.

"Actually," Adam said, waving me over. "This is Jolie, Mom. You remember her."

"Ah yes," she said, looking at me like I was a piece of meat that had gone bad. "The little working girl who used to get you into so much trouble."

I waited for her to smile but she didn't.

Adam's eyes were apologetic when he turned to me. "Jolie, this is my mother."

I stuck my hand out.

She looked at my hand like it was covered in shit, clasped her gloved fingers together, and then tilted one hand towards the younger woman. "And this is Victoria, Adam's fiancée."

My heart stopped.

"She's not my fiancée," Adam said.

"It's true," Victoria said, her voice deeper than I would've guessed. "He hasn't asked yet."

"A minor detail," his mother said, rolling her eyes. "You're as good as engaged as far as I'm concerned."

"Do you have a reservation?" I asked, my gag reflex twitching.

"We're not even dating," Adam said.

His mother pulled a white glove off and placed a hand on his forehead. "I think the heat is getting to you, dear. Perhaps you should have a seat."

I glanced at him, letting him see the hurt in my eyes and regretting it immediately.

"We've already checked in," his mother said without looking at me. "It's just a matter of our bags."

I felt the blood drain from my head. "I'll have them taken to your roo-"

"You'll do no such thing," Adam said, putting his hand on my shoulder.

I shrugged it off and stepped back. "If you insist," I said, not looking at him again. "Nice meeting both of you." My voice was on the verge of cracking. "I hope you have a pleasant stay."

"Jolie." He grabbed my wrist as I walked away.

"What are you doing?" I asked, pulling my hand back.

His dark eyes looked desperate. "This isn't what it looks like."

"I'm sure it's none of my business," I said, my chest burning. "Good evening."

I could feel his eyes on me as I walked down the hall. I wasn't sure where I was going exactly, but I knew I needed to get away from the women who'd just shown up and pissed all around Adam before looking at me like I did it.

My hands were shaking so bad by the time I got to the parking lot I dropped my keys twice before deciding to walk home.

It must've taken me at least half an hour to make the trip but it didn't feel it. On the contrary, the fire in my legs propelled me forward so effortlessly that I walked into traffic twice without looking, not even realizing what I'd done until the honks and the flashing lights of the irritated drivers got my attention.

And the whole time, all I could think about was how stupid I'd been.

Why would I ever think a guy like that would go for a girl like me?

Even if I indulged myself enough to believe that his feelings for me had been genuine- that he hadn't just been slumming it with a girl from the other side of the tracks- it was ridiculous to ignore the social pressures he'd grown up with.

Under no circumstance was Adam Darling ever going to end up with a girl who'd never left the country, a girl who'd never been to college, and a girl who could be seduced by nothing more than a takeout calzone and a free night under the stars.

It was a joke.

And I could see that now.

He'd been taking what he wanted his whole life, and I'd only managed to get on his list of to do's because I played hard to get when he first showed up.

But it was all a game, and I was a fool for playing it.

Worst of all, who knows how long I would've let him lead me on, how far I would've fallen, and how stupid I would've looked in the end when he disappeared as quickly as he'd arrived?

After all, the Prince never falls for Cinderella in real life.

Just like Adam Darling would only fall for me if this were a fairytale.

And it wasn't.

And while there was no denying that my evening with him had been a dream come true, it was obvious that there would be no happily ever after.

THIRTY
- Adam -

I was so livid I could taste blood, and as soon as Jolie walked out, I was ready to start flipping tables in my own goddamn lobby.

Unwilling to let my staff hear the things that were going through my mind, I got my mom and Victoria's bags to their rooms. Then I watched with folded arms as Victoria helped my mom take her cocktail of medications before kissing her good night.

Fortunately for my mother, she was too fragile for me to make a scene so late, but I figured the least I could do was make sure Victoria had a plane ticket home before I called it a night.

Hazel Kelly

She pulled the door to my mom's room closed as if there were a sleeping baby inside instead of a woman on a Kindle. "So how about that drink?" she asked.

"I've got some whiskey in my room," I said, turning down the hall.

"But I don't drink whis-"

"You can have whatever's in the mini bar," I said, waving a hand in the air. "I need a whiskey."

She followed me as best she could, though I knew I was walking too fast to accommodate her sky high heels.

When we reached my room, I swiped my keycard, opened the door for her, and flicked the light on as she went inside.

"The hotel is lovely," she said.

I went straight to the mini bar. "What do you want? Vodka? Gin?"

"Vodka's fine," she said, sitting on the small couch like her tailored skirt wasn't really meant to be sat in. "With cranberry juice if-"

"No mixers," I said, tossing the small liquor bottle towards her.

She caught it but made a face like I'd hit her.

I opened the cupboard above the mini bar, removed a half empty liter of Black Bush, and poured myself a double.

"So who was that girl?"

"Jolie," I said, wondering where she'd gone and if she was okay.

She furrowed her thin brows. "I assumed that wasn't her real name."

"Well, it is. And I'm in love with her." I took a sip of the whiskey and walked to the chair opposite the couch.

"I beg your pardon?" Victoria said, setting the small vodka bottle on the glass table between us.

"I wish you'd beg my forgiveness," I said. "Because I have half a mind to strangle you."

"Is this how you talk now? Like a genuine hillbilly? After just a few weeks down here?"

"Why are you here?" I leaned forward and dropped my head, trying to push Jolie's face from my mind so I wouldn't have to imagine the hurt she was feeling. "You and I both know I didn't invite you dow-"

"Did you say you're in love with her?"

I stared at the crème colored carpet between my feet. "That's right."

"But she's... she's..."

I lifted my eyes. "What?"

"Not good enough for you."

I squinted. "You mean not rich enough?"

"Obviously."

"I know this is going to sound crazy to you, but that's not a problem for me."

She pressed her dark lips together. "Do you have a fever or something? Because if I didn't know better, I'd think you were deliberately trying to hurt my feelings."

I sighed. "Hurting your feelings has never been my intention, Vic, but you're acting like a crazy person. Haven't you any pride at all?"

"Pride?"

I sat up and leaned back in my chair. "I don't love you, and I don't want to spend my life with you. You have to stop this charade."

"The only charade is you gallivanting around like we didn't have a deal."

"We didn't."

"Fine," she said. "Plans. Whatever. We had plans."

I raised a hand and rubbed my eyes.

"Our fathers are business associates. Our families get along. We both have excellent genes and similar backgrounds. And we want the same things."

"No we don't."

She turned her palms towards the ceiling. "What are you talking about? Of course we do."

I shook my head. "No. I want to marry someone I love, and you don't."

"Yes I do."

"Oh please. You don't love me, Victoria. You love how easy it would be to merge our lives."

"There are a lot of different kinds of love, Adam."

"And you deserve more."

"There isn't more."

"Yes there is," I said. "Don't you want to wake up next to someone who can't believe his luck that he's with you? Someone who thinks you're the most clever, charming, beautiful woman on the planet and counts down the minutes when you're apart?"

She looked at her lap. "That's not going to happen for me."

"Why not? You're a fantastic catch. You're a wonderful cook, you always look amazing, and no one throws a better party."

"True."

I raised my eyebrows. "You're maternal and kind and dependable."

She blinked at me.

"There's a man out there that could love the shit out of you," I said. "It's just not me, and you can't meet him as long as you allow yourself to remain hung up on what we had, which was never anything but a relationship of convenience and you know it."

"And what if I don't?" she asked. "What if I don't find someone like that?"

I opened my mouth to speak.

"Then I'll have nothing," she said. "I'll be a rich, lonely spinster with no one to leave my money, my recipes, or my property, too, and everything I've worked for- everything my parents have worked for- will have been a waste."

I pressed my lips together.

"My whole family is counting on me," she said. "Don't you get that? My sister married a PE teacher. It's all down to me now."

"Hold on a second," I said, stepping around the table and sitting beside her.

She sighed.

"You're forgetting something."

"What?"

"Your sister," I said, turning my knees towards her. "She's happy, isn't she?"

"The happiest person I know," she said, nodding. "Though I can't imagine why."

"You know exactly why."

"Because she cracked under pressure and lost her mind?"

I laughed. "No, Vic. Because she followed her heart."

"So?"

I set my drink down. "So your parents didn't disown her."

"No."

"And they didn't ban Doug from family functions."

"Of course not."

"And they still spoil her kids so rotten that they're all entitled little shits."

Her eyes bugged out.

"I was just trying to see if you were paying attention."

"It's only the eldest that's precocious."

"I was joking," I said. "Do you see where I'm going with this, though?"

"You think I should marry a gym teacher?"

"No. I think you need to recognize the fact that the kind of money your family has isn't going to disappear overnight because you did or didn't end up with a specific person."

Her dark eyes looked sad.

"You have to loosen up," I said, "and stop living in fear."

She craned her neck back. "Fear?"

I nodded.

"I'm not afraid of anything."

"Yes you are. You're afraid of anything that can't be predicted by economic advisors, and that includes romantic feelings."

"What would I even say though?" she said. "If people thought you broke up with me, who would even want-"

"Lots of people," I said. "And you don't have to tell them that's what happened. Say I started blowing money on ridiculous investments and you got out just before I dragged you down with me."

She raised her eyebrows. "Yeah?"

"Or say you didn't love me. Your family will understand."

"What about your mom?" she asked.

"What about her?"

"She needs me."

"No she doesn't," I said. "She needs a good doctor and a few people she can manipulate, and you don't need to be one of the latter anymore."

"I like her, though."

"I know, and if you don't want to cut off all ties, I understand. But you have to stop pretending there's anything between you and me."

She looked down at her clasped hands. "But I'm a terrible flirt, and I can never tell if guys are genuine. At least with you I never had to worry you were just after my money."

"There are worse problems to have Vic."

"Like what?" she asked.

"Like being in love with someone and knowing that when you tell them, they might not believe you."

THIRTY ONE
- Jolie -

I couldn't remember the last time I felt so strung out, and if the look on Gia's face when she saw me walk into the staff kitchen was anything to go by, I looked as bad as I felt.

"Are you okay?" Her eyes glanced at the clock on the wall. "What are you even doing here?"

"I need to talk to you before water aerobics."

"Really?" she asked. "You look like you should've chosen your beauty rest instead."

"Please," I said, lowering my voice so as not to disturb the other early shifters. "In private."

She set the coffee pot back on its stand.

"You should bring that," I said.

"But then there will only be decaf."

"Did I stutter?" I asked, my every blink scratching my dry eyes.

Gia made replacing the coffee someone else's problem while I grabbed a mug from the cupboard. Then she followed me to a far corner of the pool deck, which was deserted at such an early hour.

"You're freaking me out," she said, pouring me some coffee once we'd sat on a plastic lounge chair.

"I'm freaking me out, too," I said. "That's why I'm here so early. So you can talk me down from this place."

"What happened?"

"I need you to swear on your life that you'll keep everything I tell you between us."

"My life isn't worth much," she said. "Would you rather I swear on Zac Efron's life?"

A smile broke through my face. It had been less than twelve hours since I let one out, but it felt like it had been so long my cheeks might crumble like dried plaster from moving that way. "As long as you respect that someone will die if you don't keep the following to yourself."

"Fine," she said. "Then I'll swear on my life just in case because I feel like Zac Efron still has so much to give."

I raised my eyebrows. "Can we stop talking about Zac for two seconds?"

"Yeah, sorry. I just watched *17 Again* last night and that movie always-"

"I slept with Adam."

Her dark eyes grew wide. "Adam Adam?"

I nodded.

"That's amazing! I knew you would come to your senses."

"Shh!" I looked over my shoulder. The pool area was still deserted apart from a lap swimmer that had slipped in the water undetected.

"We should celebrate," she whispered.

"There won't be any celebrating."

She furrowed her brows. "Why?"

I stared over the dunes to where elderly couples walked hand in hand along the shore as young people with covetous bodies jogged past them in the warm morning sun. The image of Adam in his running shorts flashed through my mind.

"Jolie." Gia knocked her shoulder into mine. "Wake up."

"Sorry. What was I saying?"

"You were trying to explain why we shouldn't celebrate the fact that you got laid."

"Oh right." I looked into my mug.

"Was it not good or something?"

"It's not that," I said, tucking some hair behind my ear. "It was amazing."

"It's starting to sound like you should be telling your diary about it and not me."

"First of all, I don't have a diary," I said. "And second of all, the problem is that it was too good to be true."

"Did he go all porno on you or something?"

My eyes grew wide.

"I could see him being kinky behind closed doors."

"Jesus, Gia. What the hell? No. It's nothing like that."

"So why isn't this a happy story?"

I sighed. "Because there's someone else."

"What?" She craned her neck forward. "How could there be? He doesn't even know anyone besides that one couple and the staff. Please tell me it's not Debbie's daughter. I knew that floozy was trouble."

"I wish it was a floozy."

"So who is it?" she asked.

"Some rich girl from home who looks like she could be royalty compared to me."

"Okaaay."

"She showed up here with his mother last night."

Her mouth fell open.

"And now they're staying here."

Gia looked over her shoulder like we'd been dropped behind enemy lines.

"So I'm essentially paralyzed with mortification."

"Did you meet them?" she asked, drinking from her mug.

"Yeah. They were in the lobby when we got back from our date last night, and Adam was clearly freaked out, like he'd been caught in a web of lies."

"What did he do?"

"Introduced me to them super awkwardly before I dismissed myself because I thought I was going to throw up."

"Did he come after you?" she asked. "Did he even try to explain?"

I shook my head. "I feel like such a fool."

"You shouldn't. It's not your fault he lied to you."

"I should've listened to my gut," I said. "I should've kept my wits about me instead of shitting on my own doorstep."

"You know I would key his car for you in any other situation, but the guy's my boss and-"

"I know. Don't worry about it. I'm not interested in retaliating. If anything, that would only highlight what a naïve tool I am."

"You're not a tool," she said. "And you're not the first woman on the planet who's been lied to by a broad shouldered man with smoldering eyes."

I glared at her.

"What?"

"That's not helping."

She scrunched her face. "Sorry. So now what?"

"I just want to lay low as best I can. But if you catch me scowling at anyone or nothing, I need you to elbow me in the ribs."

"That I can do," she said. "But I'm not sure you should even work today?"

"I have to work. I have to keep up appearances."

"No you don't," she said. "You should take the day off. I'll say you're having lady problems or something."

"First of all, this is my job, not eighth grade gym class. Second of all, things went a little too far last night for that to be believable. And last but not least, I'm not having lady problems. I'm having man problems."

"I'm so sorry, Jolie. I thought he was different."

"Me too."

She scooted over and put her arm around me.

I dropped my head on her shoulder. "I thought we could pick up where we left off. I actually let myself believe we were fated or something."

"I kind of thought you were, too," she said. "But hey, look on the bright side."

I lifted my face. "What bright side?"

"At least you found out what kind of guy he is sooner rather than later."

I bit the inside of my cheek.

"So it'll be easy to get over him now."

I dropped my head on her shoulder again, closed my eyes, and wished with everything that I actually believed that.

THIRTY TWO
- Adam -

I wheeled the breakfast trolley up to my mom's door and knocked.

She opened it with a smile, looking all made up like she'd been awake for ages with the morning newspaper hanging from one hand.

"Hello, my darling," she said, pressing her cheek to mine once I'd wheeled the trolley in. "I could've managed the buffet, you know? I'm not an invalid quite yet."

"It's no trouble, Mom. Having you here is a treat for me, too."

"Will Victoria be joining us?" she asked, sitting on a cushioned chair while I laid out the plates.

"No. Victoria went home."

Her eyes grew wide. "Pardon?"

"I arranged for a car to take her to the airport this morning so she could catch the first flight back to New York."

"But I need her here."

"No you don't," I said, laying a napkin across her lap. "And I don't want her here. She's not my girlfriend anymore, and she's never going to be my fiancée."

"But she knows all about my treatments and-"

"She's had enough," I said, setting a plate of unsalted scrambled eggs down in front of her. "You've been taking advantage of her kindness and it's not appropriate."

"But-"

"I've arranged for a nurse to be on call for the rest of your visit, and she'll accompany you back to New York when you're ready."

She puckered her heavily lined lips. "This isn't exactly turning into the warm welcome I was expecting."

"Well, you shouldn't have come," I said. "You know you're not supposed to travel, and frankly, the way you spoke to Jolie last night really pissed me off." I uncovered a cheesy omelet for myself.

"What on Earth- who's Jolie?"

"The woman I was with last night."

"The staff member?"

"This is her hotel," I said. "And the way you treated her was embarrassing for everyone."

"I thought it was your hotel," she said, pouring herself a cup of tea. "Didn't you buy it?"

"It's mine on paper, but it's her hotel. It belonged to her parents back when we used to come here."

A light went on behind her eyes. "Ah yes, Jolie. I thought she looked familiar." She waved a frail hand at me. "Do tell her I apologize then. I didn't mean to offend anyone."

"You can apologize to her yourself," I said. "And while you're at it, you can tell her you didn't mean any of the nonsense you spat last night about me and Victoria."

She dropped her chin and covered her chest with one hand. "I really don't think I'm up to such a thing."

"Bullshit. If you can get on a plane just to come stick your nose in my business, you can suck it up and apologize to the woman I love."

"Well of course I'll be apologizing to Victoria. You've obviously forgotten yourself in dismissing her so unceremoniously."

"Cut the crap, Mom. I'm not buying it anymore. You're not the frail old lady you pretend to be, and you're not a victim here."

"I beg your pardon?"

"I gave it a shot with Victoria," I said, taking a seat across from her. "Really, I did. I knew it was what you wanted, and I tried to make it work, but I don't love her." I pulled the cuffs of my white shirt down. "And she doesn't love me either. So we're not going to waste our time anymore."

"But all I ever wanted was for you to-"

"Do exactly what you wanted. I know. But I can't marry someone I don't love. It's not in me to do that. I know people who've settled and who've gone along with their parent's wishes, and I admit some of them are happy."

Her mouth pursed like a drawstring pouch.

"But I'm in love with someone else, and I have been since I was a teenager."

She raised a palm between us. "Please don't tell me that working class girl I met last night is the woman you're alluding to."

"It is."

She clutched her chest.

I rolled my eyes and leaned back against the couch.

"I hope you haven't told her that yet."

"Actually, I haven't. But I plan to very soon."

She shook her head and blinked slowly. "I understand if you want to have a fling with her, honey. I've lived long enough to know sometimes men have to do that sort of thing before they can settle down with someone appropriate, but have you considered the wide reaching implications it would have if you really wanted to be with a girl like that?"

"I haven't the slightest idea what you're referring to."

"Well you can't take her anywhere," she said. "She's probably never had an etiquette class in her life."

"So what?"

"So she'd stick out like a sore thumb no matter where you invited her."

"I'm pretty sure I could tell her which fork to use and how to hold the stem of her glass if that's what it would take for you to accept her."

"It's not that simple, Adam, and you know it. It all comes down to breeding, and it wouldn't be fair to her to put her in those situations which you can't avoid. She wouldn't be comfortable."

"If I never go to a stuffy party again it will be too soon. Everyone's always so worried about putting a foot or the corner of their napkin wrong, they're not even fun."

"Even so," she said, lifting her saucer into her lap and gripping the thin handle of her teacup. "She'd run you into the ground."

"What?"

"She'd go crazy as soon as she had access to your money. I guarantee it."

I scoffed. "You're wrong. Only women that don't appreciate hard work are capable of that. And that's not Jolie. She has simple tastes and enjoys the little things. She doesn't even care about my money."

"Do you really believe that?"

"I do."

She tutted. "I blame myself for making you so naïve about women. They're wiley, Adam. Especially the ones that have had to be to survive."

I was ready to pull my hair out. "Why can't you just be happy for me?"

"Because your happiness with this girl can only be fleeting, and it's your long term happiness that concerns me."

"In that case, I'd like you to leave."

She stared across the table. "Excuse me?"

"If you can't treat me and the woman I love with respect, I don't want you here. There are enough obstacles to making it work without you buzzing negativity in my ear and making her feel like she's not good enough."

"Now you're being hasty."

"There are two flights this afternoon, both of which have first class seats available."

"Stop, Adam. I get it."

I tilted an ear towards her.

"I can see that you're serious about this girl and that you won't be persuaded."

"Go on."

"And I understand that Victoria wasn't wild enough to hold your interest."

I groaned. "I swear to god if you even say her name again-"

"Forgive me." She laid her hands in her lap. "The last thing I want is for you to feel like I don't support you or like I wish you anything but happiness and love."

I clenched my jaw.

"I want to make amends."

I took a deep breath.

"If you'll allow it, I'd like to have Jolie up to my room for tea this afternoon."

I narrowed my eyes at her.

"So I can get to know her better, just the two of us," she said, her voice as warm as her expression. "The least I can do is give her a chance."

"Really?"

"Of course," she said. "I know when I've been beaten. And if she's as dear to you as you say, then it's only right that I give her the apology she deserves before I head back to New York."

"That would mean a lot to me, Mom," I said, feeling like I'd finally gotten through. "And I'm sure it would mean a lot to her, too."

She smiled and cocked her head. "Then it would be my pleasure."

THIRTY THREE
- Jolie -

According to the booking system, the only Victoria staying with us had checked out that morning. Meanwhile, Mrs. Annette Darling had ordered room service for two.

To say I desperately wanted to know what was going on was an understatement, but I wasn't about to ask. What would I even say?

All the questions that sprang to mind were too pathetically sad.

Did last night mean nothing to you? Why did you lie to me? Why are you even here? Just to destroy my life?

Each one made me sound more and more like I was starring in my own pathetic Lifetime movie- and not one of the happy ones that makes you feel so good you don't even care how badly acted it is.

On the contrary, my life right now was one of those sad ones that makes you wish you weren't even a woman because of how doomed you are to feel everything so deeply until the day death puts you out of your misery.

Ugh.

Perhaps I shouldn't drink coffee when I'm depressed. After all, it wasn't actually making me feel better. All it did was make the depressing thoughts spin through my mind faster.

My only saving grace was that I knew Adam was going to be in meetings in the south wing all morning so at least he wouldn't see me looking such a mess.

"Hey," Gia said, walking up to the desk in her work clothes with her hair in an updo.

I glanced at the clock. "You're getting faster," I said, referring to a conversation we'd had a week prior about how the point of water aerobics wasn't to make her super late for reception duty.

"I'm trying," she said, walking around the counter. "Feeling any better than you were earlier?"

"You know that saying, if you don't have anything nice to say-"

"Got it."

"Actually," I said, raising a finger. "That's not entirely true."

"Oh?" She opened her purse and rummaged through it.

"The alleged fiancée checked out this morning."

She raised her eyebrows. "Already?"

I nodded.

She pulled her lipstick out and lifted her eyes. "That's weird."

"I know."

"Any idea what happened?" she asked before painting her lips a deep red.

"No, but I'm relieved to have one less person to be embarrassed around."

She nodded as she reached for the ringing phone. "Good morning, this is Gia. How can I help you?"

I drummed my nails on the marble desk.

Her eyes flashed at me. "Who should I say is calling?"

Out of the corner of my eye, I watched a kid slathered in half absorbed sunscreen follow his mom outside.

Gia lowered the phone and covered it with her palm. "It's Mrs. Darling."

"What does she want?"

"To talk to you."

I tried to swallow, but my mouth had gone dry.

She held out the phone.

"Jolie speaking."

"Hello, Jolie. This is Adam's mother."

I wondered if she was calling with her white gloves on. "What can I do for you?"

"I was wondering if you might join me in my room for a cup of tea?"

My lips fell apart.

"I realize you're working, but I won't take much of your time."

I glanced at the clock. "When did you-?"

"The sooner the better," she said. "Please bring a pot of black, cream if you take it."

I stared at the phone. "She hung up."

"What did she say?"

"She wants me to join her for a cup of tea."

Gia shook her head. "Rich people are so weird."

"I don't think I want to go."

"You have to," she said. "It's your boss's mom."

"Yeah, but-"

"Just focus on that and put everything else out of your mind," she said. "And if you're not back in twenty minutes, I'll call with some sort of catering emergency or something."

I blinked at her.

"Go." She shooed me away with her hand.

"Okay," I said, smoothing my hair back. "Jeez."

It took me a few minutes to get the tray of tea ready, but I was knocking on her door before ten minutes had passed.

"Jolie, hello," she said, opening the door and extending her hand towards the coffee table.

I forced a smile and set the tray down, doing my best not to invade her privacy by letting my eyes wander around the room

She closed the door. "Please have a seat."

I did as I was told and watched her move towards the seat across from me. She seemed slower this morning, and while her face was still eerily devoid of wrinkles, her skin wasn't a healthy color.

When she perched at the edge of her chair, I noticed that the nightstand across the room was covered with nearly a dozen pill bottles.

"So," she said, nodding at the tea between us.

"Oh, sorry." I leaned forward and filled both our cups.

"I suppose you're wondering why I asked you to come."

"Is it that obvious?" I said, trying to lighten the mood.

Her mouth twitched, but she didn't smile. "Firstly, I wanted to apologize."

I raised my eyebrows.

"I realize the way I spoke to you last night when you were off the clock was inappropriate."

"That's alright," I said. "You were just eager to get settled in your room after a long day of traveling. I completely understand."

"I also apologize for introducing Victoria as Adam's fiancée."

I raised my cup to my lips.

"Apparently I was mistaken."

The hot tea singed my taste buds.

"Turns out he doesn't love her."

I singed them again.

"It was wishful thinking on my part," she said. "It has always been a dream of mine that he would settle down with a woman who was of a similar pedigree. You know, someone from a family with money so his assets would be secure. Someone well-traveled. And educated, obviously."

"I see."

"Victoria has two master's degrees," she continued. "And her family have been dear friends of ours for many years."

I nodded and put my cup down on the saucer.

"Anyway, it seems my dream for him has become sort of a dying wish," she said, her eyes glassy. "Only God knows if he'll find someone worthy of him before I pass."

"Pardon me, Mrs. Darling, but I'm not sure what point you're trying to make."

"Oh right," she said, her eyes clearing as she fixed them on me. "My point is, I misspoke. He doesn't love her."

"I see, well-"

"But he doesn't love you either."

I turned an ear towards her. "What?"

"It breaks my heart to tell you that, but from one woman to another, I can't let you be blindsided."

I furrowed my brow. "I don't understand."

"He's just having fun with you, Jolie. It's not serious. It never can be."

I bit the inside of my cheek.

"When he confided in me that you merely made for a convenient distraction down here, it angered me that he wasn't showing you more respect."

I shook my head.

"I tried to tell him that it was unfair to lead you on, unfair to let you imagine what your life might be like with him long term," she said. "But he insisted you were lucky that he showed you any attention at all considering the type of men you usually go out with."

I clenched my jaw.

"He's always been terribly arrogant that way," she said, laying a hand on her chest. "And I blame myself. I really do. It's not right for him to manipulate you when you're so vulnerable."

I opened my mouth.

"He would be mortified if he knew I were telling you this, of course," she said, shaking her head. "He's never approved of me butting into his affairs, but I had to warn you."

My chest tightened.

She cocked her head. "He's planning on stringing you along until the very end, and I could tell by the way he said it that he's not taking your feelings into account at all."

"Right."

"I'm sorry to be the bearer of bad news," she said, laying her hands on her thin thighs. "But I don't have much time left on this planet, and I've got to make every play for Heaven that I can."

"I understand," I said, standing up.

Then I made an excuse to leave and braced myself against the wall in the hallway, wishing I'd had the guts to ask her for some sedatives on my way out.

THIRTY FOUR
- Adam -

"Can I grab you for a second?" I asked, laying my fingers on the edge of the front desk.

Gia blanked me like she'd never seen me before in her life, and Jolie didn't lift her eyes from the computer.

"Jolie."

She looked at me.

"Did you hear me?" I asked.

"Sorry," she said, her hands poised over the keyboard. "What can I do for you?"

"I want to show you the renovated suite," I said. "Carrie's put all the finishing touches on it, and I need your go ahead before she can roll out the rest."

"I'd be happy to make some time to look at it," she said. "When did you want-"

"Now," I said. "I want you to come look at it now."

Jolie looked at Gia, who nodded once without looking at me again.

No matter how slow I walked, I couldn't get Jolie to stay beside me as we headed down the hall to the elevators.

"I trust your mother had a pleasant stay?" she asked as I pushed the elevator call button.

"My mom rarely has a pleasant anything these days, but I believe she did."

"Good."

"I understand she had a chance to apologize to you?" I clasped my hands in front of me. "About the whole misunderstanding with Victoria?"

"She did."

The elevator dinged, and I held the door open for her.

She stepped inside.

Hazel Kelly

"Is everything okay?" I asked, stepping up to her after the doors closed.

"Everything's fine," she said, seeming distracted. "I just have a lot on my mind."

"I'm not sure how that's even possible," I said. "I can't think about anything besides the other night."

She stepped around me, and walked out the open doors onto the executive floor. "So will you be moving into the suite?" she asked. "Should I have someone collect your things?"

"No," I said, pulling my keycard from my pocket as we walked down the hall. "I can move myself. I don't have much."

Something was wrong. My mind knew it, but my body was too fixated on getting her alone again, on smelling her, tasting her, having her touch my-

"Wow," she said, her eyes popping open as she stepped into the newly renovated suite.

I closed the door behind her and watched her move to the middle of the room.

"This is incredible," she said, sliding open the door to the redecorated balcony.

324

"I think we can charge at least double for this room now."

"I'll say," she said, her eyes sweeping across the patio furniture and then straight out to the beach. "It's so private up here."

"I'm glad you like it."

She walked around me and went back into the room, bringing a breeze with her that shifted the sheer curtains hanging on each corner of the new four poster bed.

I stuck a hand in my pocket. "By the time we're finished, I want all the rooms to feel this luxurious."

"It was hard to imagine this when all I saw were tiny swatches of fabrics and paints, but this is really beautiful." She ran her hand along the bedspread before lifting her eyes towards the polished seashells on the bedside tables.

"I'm so glad you like it," I said, sliding my hands around her waist.

She froze in my arms.

"There's only one problem," I said, dragging my day old stubble up her neck before kissing her earlobe.

"What's that?" she asked, lowering her voice.

"The place needs to be christened," I said, sliding the zipper on her skirt down.

"Adam."

"Shhhh." I pushed her skirt to the floor and squeezed the plump cheek of her ass. "Wanting you is all I can think about," I said, pressing my hard-on against her. "Don't deny me the pleasure of making you come again."

She turned her face towards me.

"I needed to have you yesterday, and it was like the whole world was conspiring against me." I slid a hand between her cheeks and pressed my fingertips against her slit.

"It's office hours," she said. "This isn't right."

"It's the only thing that's right." I pulled her thong down and found her heat again.

She arched her ass towards me.

"Take your shirt off," I growled in her ear.

I watched over her shoulder as she unfastened each button, allowing the shape of her breasts to become visible.

By the time she pulled her shirt off over her head, my mouth was watering.

I undid her white lace bra with one hand and reached around to grope her perfect tits until she grew wet enough for me to slip my fingers inside her.

"Adam," she moaned.

The sound of my name on her lips made me drive into her deeper. "God you're so wet for me," I said, my hunger for her increasing as her pussy clenched around my thick fingers.

I needed to be inside her, needed to make her mine all over again. I undid my pants and pushed them down as best I could with one hand.

Her breath hitched in her throat as I pulled my fingers from her and wiped her sweet nectar on my cock, staring at her ass as I stroked myself.

She was about to turn around when I grabbed her hips and squared up to her. "Bend over," I said, guiding myself to her dripping slit.

She leaned a bit, but when I plunged inside her, she fell forward and gripped the white comforter.

I rocked my hips against her, a feeling of insatiable lust overwhelming me as her pussy choked my throbbing cock. When her knuckles turned white, I slowed down.

"Oh god," she moaned. "That feels too good."

I rubbed my wet fingertips together and massaged the rim of her asshole, watching the delicate muscles in her back twitch as I spread her open with every thrust.

When I realized she was sliding farther onto the bed, I stopped teasing her rim and lifted her thighs so I could drive myself even further inside her.

"I'm coming," she stuttered over the sound of my slapping balls.

As soon her pussy began to pulse, I pulled out of her and dropped to my knees, dragging her hips towards me and clamping my open mouth over her wet slit so I could swallow her pleasure down.

When her body stopped shaking and went limp, I stopped to catch my breath, sitting back on my heels and giving her ass a firm slap.

Then I pulled my shirt off over my head, threw it to the side, and stood up.

I admired the way her perfect body was draped over the edge of bed, letting my eyes travel past the dip in her lower back, past her tapered waist, and up to where her toned back was rising and falling with her breath.

Then I flipped her over.

Her flushed face stared up at mine for a moment before her eyes dropped to my swollen cock.

I smoothed my hands up her thighs and curled them around her hipbones. "Your pussy is to die for."

THIRTY FIVE
- Jolie -

I still wanted him with every part of me, and I was too exhausted to pretend I didn't.

Obviously it occurred to me that I should stop him.

And I'd tried to be cold, tried to revert back to my old standoffishness.

But I guess I wasn't very convincing.

How could I be?

When he came up behind me smelling so irresistibly masculine and dragged his stubble up my neck, I couldn't move much less pretend my body wasn't craving him back.

Besides, maybe it could just be about sex for me, too?

How could I know if I didn't give it a chance?

But I knew as I laid there on my back with him standing naked between my legs that I was fucked in more ways than one.

Because there was no way I could use this guy, no way I could pretend it was just about his body, no way I could stop myself from wanting more with him, imagining more with him.

And it was foolish to do so.

Fortunately for me, I was too dumb to realize that before I got myself into this mess and now I was too weak with longing to speak up about it.

So I would indulge him one last time, and I would enjoy myself. Because I deserved to get fucked in a good way for a change, and it was about time I got what I wanted, even if it was only for a few minutes.

I scooted back on the bed, drinking in the rippling abs that lead to the most delicious cock I'd ever sucked... which was attached to the biggest dick I'd ever known. "Come and get it," I said, flashing my eyebrows at him.

Adam crawled onto the end of the bed, his tan body a vision in the white room. "I'm fucking crazy about you," he said, moving over me with a predatory look in his eyes.

I decided to act like I believed him for just a few more minutes.

He kissed my lips so softly I wanted to cry. It was easier when I couldn't see him, when I couldn't see the expression on his face as he used me.

I reached for his dick and stroked it, squeezing it as hard as I could before guiding it inside me.

He looked me in the eyes as he sank inside.

"Fuck, Jolie. You feel too good."

"Deeper," I said, grabbing his ass and tilting my hips up.

He hit me where no one ever had before, but he moved slower than I wanted him to, as if he knew I were trying to memorize the feel of every glorious inch of him.

"How's that?" he asked, his hips rocking as his eyes dropped to my lips.

"Harder," I said, wishing he wouldn't pretend this meant something. "I want you to fuck me."

He clenched his jaw and sped up the pace.

I furrowed my brow and looked down past his flexing chest to where his dark cock was sliding in and out of me.

A moment later, he grabbed one of my bent legs and pushed my thigh right up against my chest, hitting me so deep I cried out and squeezed my eyes shut.

A low growl escaped his throat as he exploded, his dick surging as he filled me.

And despite my best efforts not to care, I burned the moment to the back of my eyelids, knowing I would think of it in the future when I touched myself and when I fucked other guys.

Because even though I couldn't do this to myself anymore, I knew he was the best I'd ever have.

He always was.

I listened to his breath as he panted in my ear, savoring the way the cool ocean breeze flowed over my warm limbs where they stuck out beneath him.

"That was fucking amazing," he said finally, rolling onto his side.

I turned my head to admire him one last time, letting my eyes consume every inch of his gorgeous body and his handsome, chiseled face.

His gaze dropped to my seahorse, and he dragged a thumb over it before sliding his palm across my chest to squeeze my breasts again.

I had to hand it to the guy. He did know how to make a woman feel like a goddess.

He dragged his hand down and rested it on my stomach for a second before twirling my dangly belly button ring around his finger like a distracted school boy. Then he propped his head up on his bottom arm and fixed his eyes on mine. "I love you, Jolie."

The rose colored lenses I'd been looking through turned gray. "What?"

"I love you."

"No you don't," I said, sitting up. "Don't say that."

He sat up. "Hey."

I scooted to the side of the bed.

"I knew it was a bit optimistic to hope you'd say it too, but-"

I bent over and started scooping up my clothes.

"What's the problem?" he asked. "You think it's too soon?"

I set my clothes on the end of the bed and grabbed my underwear first. "More like too ridiculous."

"What are you talking about?" He scooted to the end of the bed. "Why are you getting dressed?"

"Because this was about sex," I said, fastening my bra. "And the sex is over."

He shook his head. "What? What are you talking about?"

"I thought I could do this," I said. "I really did, but I can't go along with it anymore."

"You're not making any sense, Jo. We just had a good time." He lifted a palm. "Slow down."

"You're my boss, and I got distracted, but this isn't me. I'm sorry." I pulled my shirt on and started doing up the buttons as fast as I could.

"What are you saying?"

"I'm saying I don't love you back," I said, unable to look at him. "And that's not going to change."

He swung his feet over the edge of the bed.

"So rather than string you along, I'm going to wish you well and keep my legs shut from now on."

"String me along?" He furrowed his brow. "I don't want you to keep your legs shut!"

I grabbed my skirt. "I guess you can't always get what you want after all."

"Was it something I said?" He stood on the floor and turned towards me. "Is this really happening?"

"It's nothing you said." I stepped into my skirt. "You've been saying all the right things since you got here. If anything, that's what's caused this whole problem."

He grabbed my shoulders. "What problem?"

I sighed. "The problem of me going against my better judgement."

He bent down to look me in the eyes.

I wiggled away from him. "It was unfair of me to take advantage of-"

"You haven't taken advantage. I'm a grown man."

"A grown man who'll be happier with someone else," I said, my voice nearly cracking.

"What's gotten into you?" he asked. "Was it my mom? Victoria? They're gone now."

I shook my head while I tucked in my shirt. "I'm just not up for this anymore, okay? Haven't you ever been rejected before?"

"Jolie-"

"Now would be a good time to put your clothes on."

"But I'm only here for you."

"See," I said, zipping my skirt. "That's a perfect example of the kind of ridiculous stuff you don't have to say anymore."

"But it's true."

"No it's not," I said, fixing my hair. "You're here for the hotel."

"That's not fair."

I bent over to grab my shoes but he got to them first and held them out of reach.

"Give me those," I said, putting my hand out.

"I'm here for you," he repeated.

I glared at him. "Bullshit. I'm just a curiosity who'll never be able to return your feelings."

He lowered his outstretched arm.

I raised my eyebrows. "Please give me my shoes."

"I never would've come back here if it weren't for you."

A sick taste teased the back of my throat. "That doesn't matter."

"It matters to me," he said. "A lot."

"In that case, I'm sorry. It was never my intention to hurt you."

"So you believe me at least?" he asked.

I swallowed. "I believe that if you're really only here for me then you should leave."

His dark eyes searched mine for a moment.

It took everything I had not to look away.

Then he dropped my shoes at my feet. "That'll be all Miss Monroe."

THIRTY SIX
- Adam -

I was going crazy, though not as crazy as the women in my life apparently.

Between my mom, Victoria, and Jolie, I was beginning to think I ought to be investing in straightjackets instead of startups.

Then again, I didn't really want to lump Jolie in with my mom and Vic because crazy wasn't her default setting, which was more than I could say for the other two.

But something didn't make sense.

Sure, I thought she was acting strange on the way up to the room, but I was so hell bent on seducing her again that I suppose I stopped thinking about it once we got there.

Still, she was an adult. If something was bothering her, she should've told me.

And not like that. Not then. Not when I was standing there naked with her taste on my lips.

In the space of one minute, my heart had gone from bursting with affection to throbbing with anguish, and I couldn't shake the feeling that I didn't have all the information.

Hadn't she been totally into me that night in the dunes?

Could her feelings really have changed so quickly?

It seemed impossible, but what choice did I have but to give her space? Following the incident in the suite, she froze me out and wouldn't even let me get near her.

Worst of all, my feelings hadn't changed, and despite the fact that she was treating me like an infectious disease, part of me refused to believe she didn't want me anymore.

Something else was at play. I was positive, and I had to get to the bottom of it.

Otherwise, she was right. I'd have to leave.

I couldn't stay here and not be able to touch her. Not now that I had. Not now that I was as infatuated all over again as I'd been when I was seventeen.

But I had to get my head straight, and there was only one person that could help me.

"Christophe," I said, turning up the volume on my phone. "Is this a good time?"

He laughed. "Call me tonight for a good time."

"Seriously, man. I need some advice."

"What kind?"

"I've been rejected," I said.

"Ouch."

"And I know you know all about that."

"I beg your pardon?" he asked.

"You know how you sometimes go for a girl and she rejects you, but it's not real."

"No means no, Adam."

"Unless it doesn't."

Hazel Kelly

"I'm listening," he said. "But only because this sounds like a car wreck waiting to happen."

I sighed. "A few days ago, things were going great. Then all of a sudden, I tell her I love her, and she freaks out and tells me to fuck off."

"That's hysterical."

"I'm failing to see the humor in it myself."

"First of all," he said. "Why the hell would you tell her you love her?"

"Because it's the truth, and I wanted her to know."

"What did I tell you about cooling your jets?" he asked.

"I guess I forgot and turned them back on again."

"Well that's unfortunate because you can undo some mild flirtation, but you can't take the L word back."

I scrunched my face. "I've fucked everything up, haven't I?"

"Pretty much."

"She cares about me, though. I know it."

"She has a funny way of showing it," he said.

"Can you help me or not?"

"Will she even talk to you?" he asked.

I shook my head. "Not really."

"Well, that's something."

I leaned back in my chair. "How is that good?"

"Because it makes me less convinced that she meant what she said."

I squinted. "What?"

"If she were genuinely over you, she wouldn't have to go to so much trouble to be a bitch."

"Okaay."

"She'd just be like a regular, indifferent mean girl," he said.

"I'm not sure I'm following."

"Disgust is not the opposite of love," he said. "The opposite of love is indifference."

"So what happened?" I asked. "Did I scare her off?"

"That might be it," he said. "Or it's just a classic case of self-sabotage."

"Self-sabotage?"

"Anyone's capable of it, but women are the best at it by far."

"I'm listening."

"Think about it," he continued. "If your luck's been down for as long as you can remember and then it changes, it's natural to be skeptical."

"So it's a self-preservation thing?"

"Absolutely," he said. "Say you're a recovered gambling addict who's neck deep in debt and you get a good hand."

"Uh-huh."

"Your mind will either trick you into not even realizing you've gotten lucky, or you'll register the hand and fold anyway because you're afraid to go down that path again."

"So you're saying I'm a flush?"

"I'm saying she's scared."

I scratched the back of my head. "She didn't seem scared when she told me to fuck off."

"Did she use those exact words?" he asked.

"No."

"Okay, good. Because that's a pretty clear cut sentiment, and there's not much reading into it I can do."

I sighed.

"First things first-"

I raised my eyebrows.

"Can you walk away and forget about her?"

I rolled my eyes. "If I could, would I be calling you?"

"Hey, I had to ask."

"Did you, though?"

"Sometimes it's the easiest solution."

"I can't walk away, Christophe. I love her. I want to be with her for good."

"Shit," he said. "Well that doesn't leave you with much choice."

"Go on."

"There's really only one thing you can do."

"Spit it out," I said.

"Are you willing to do whatever it takes to win her back?" he asked. "Including looking like an ass?"

"Yes, of course."

"God you didn't even have to think about it."

"Of course I didn't! I love her. Are you even paying attention?" I groaned.

"Chill, man. Hear me out."

I resisted the urge to slump in my chair. "Shoot."

"It's grand gesture time."

"What?"

"Grand gesture time," he repeated.

"What does that mean?"

"It means you have to do some big, over the top shit to get her attention and prove that you're not too good to be true."

"Soo…"

"You have to do such a good job convincing her that you're serious about her that there can be no doubt left in her mind."

"A grand gesture? That's your big idea?"

"Maybe more than one if it's necessary."

"And what if she won't give me the time of day?"

"Then you'll have to do something that doesn't require her permission."

I pressed my lips together.

"If it were up to me, I wouldn't do it right away either."

"No?"

"No," he said. "Take some time, go over your options, and let her think you're coming to terms with her bullshit."

"Why would I do that?"

"For the same reason a lioness will yawn under a tree while she watches an antelope eat grass."

I rubbed my forehead. "Still on the animal shows then?"

"Say what you want, but I leaned everything I know about timing the perfect pounce from that channel."

"You're sure about the grand gesture thing?"

"I'm sure," he said. "It's the only way."

"Is it essential that I make an ass of myself?"

"No," he said. "Just recommended."

"Right," I said, nodding. "And if it doesn't work?"

"Worst case scenario, she never forgets you."

It was a far cry from what I wanted, but I suppose it was some consolation.

After all, I sure as shit wasn't going to forget about her.

FLASHBACK
- Jolie -

I started looking for Adam as soon as I noticed his parents checking out at reception.

I found him sitting on the curb next to their stuff.

"You're leaving?" I asked.

He looked over his shoulder and stood up.

"I thought we- I thought you had another week."

"My dad's got a work thing," he said, kicking the curb. "So apparently everyone else's vacation has to get cut short, too."

I could tell he was pissed and figured piling on my own disappointment wouldn't help. "Well, it was good seeing you." *And sleeping with you under the stars and falling so hard for you I can't eat or sleep or breathe.*

"It was good seeing you, too," he said.

I glanced at the pavement between us.

"You were the highlight of my trip, Jolie."

My heart exploded in my chest.

"I really wish I didn't have to go," he said. "Or that I could bring you with me."

I smiled and tucked a sun kissed strand of hair behind my ear. "Maybe you'll come back next summer?"

He nodded. "Count on it."

I swallowed and raised my arms out.

He came in for a hug, squeezing me so tight I was worried I might not be able to hold the tears in until after he left.

"Don't ever change," he whispered in my ear.

I leaned back and looked at him, wishing with everything that we could have just one more night. "And don't you forget me."

He laughed. "Trust me. That's not going to happen."

I craned my neck forward to kiss him on the cheek, but he turned his face and pressed his lips against mine, holding the back of my head as his tongue ignited a trail of fire inside me that burned all the way down to my toes.

"Our parents are right inside," I whispered, laying a hand on his chest when I remembered where we were.

"I don't give a fuck," he said. "I already told them I wouldn't leave until I said goodbye to you."

"Yeah?"

He dropped his forehead against mine. "Of course," he said. "Except I don't think I'm going to."

"What?"

"I think I'll go with see you later."

I smiled. "I like that better, too."

"I'm going to miss that little convenience store," Christophe said to no one in particular as he walked up with two full bags of snacks. "I'm liable to go through Cheetos withdrawal once we leave here.

Adam kept his eyes on me.

"Ready to hit the road, gang?" Adam's dad asked as he walked through the lobby's double doors with his wife.

"See you later," I said, taking a step back.

Adam lifted his hand in a silent wave and watched me go back inside where I immediately turned into the shadows so I could watch his family pack up their car and drive away, as if it didn't already hurt enough.

A few minutes later, I heard my dad's voice behind me. "Nice kid."

I nodded. "Yeah."

"You're going to miss him."

I let my head fall against the wall and watched the turn signal of their rental car come on as they approached the road. "I already do."

He put his hand on my shoulder. "Do you want the good news or the bad news?"

"The good," I said. "I don't think I can handle any more bad news."

"Well." He stepped up beside me. "The good news is you're young, and you might see him again sometime."

I sighed. "And the bad?"

"You're still young, and you might not."

I rolled my eyes. "Wow, Dad. How can I ever thank you for that depressing nugget?"

"Come here," he said, gesturing for me to follow him.

I leaned off the wall.

He held out his hand.

I was too old to hold my dad's hand, but I figured I was dragging pretty low so I might as well humor him.

"You ever hear that saying, 'if you let something go and it comes back to you, it's really yours, and if you let it go and it doesn't, it wasn't meant to be anyway?'"

"I've heard a saying that goes something like that."

"Smart ass," he said, his mouth curling up into a smile.

He knew I was always surprised to hear him swear, so I assumed he was doing it to cheer me up. "What's your point?" I asked.

"My point is-" He sat down on the bench in front of the hotel and tugged my hand so I'd sit beside him. "Life is all about letting things go. Over and over. Things come into your life and then you have to let them go. Just like the waves come and go."

"So what you're saying is life's a beach?" I asked, raising my eyebrows.

He nodded. "It is, Jo. It is. And the waves keep coming and going no matter what. So you have to learn to enjoy the moment because each one is fleeting and not a single one of them is going to stick around, regardless of how tight you try and hold onto it."

"Did you already have a Bloody Mary today, Dad?"

He smiled, the sparkle in his eyes giving him away. "I need you to promise me three things, Jo."

I squinted at him. "What's the point? Aren't my promises just going to come and go like everything else?"

He raised a finger. "No. Promises are different. They're waterproof so they can't get washed away."

I shook my head. I'd been alive long enough to know that parents changed the rules as often as they saw fit, mine included. "Fine. What is it?"

"Promise me you'll look after your mother when I'm gone."

I furrowed my brow. "Where are you going?"

"Nowhere," he said. "Not anytime soon anyway. It's just that, now that you're getting a bit older, it's become apparent to me that you're stronger than she is. Or at least, you will be someday."

"Alright," I said. "If it's important to you."

"And promise you'll do what makes you happy," he said. "Because I didn't raise you to be one of those adults that drags their feet their whole life."

"What about the hotel?" I asked. "Don't you want me to promise I'll look after it?"

"Of course," he said. "But I don't want you looking after it at the expense of your own happiness. Do you understand?"

I nodded because it seemed like the right thing to do.

"As long as we keep hiring good people who take pride in their work, the hotel will take care of itself."

"Got it."

"And if you're ever struggling-" He bent over and reached between his legs under the bench.

I leaned forward too and watched as his thick fingers struggled to lift a stone tile from its place in the grout.

"What's that?" I asked when we'd righted ourselves.

He turned it over and handed it to me.

On the bottom of the cement, there was a large handprint with a tiny one inside it. "Is that-?"

"Your hand in mine," he said. "Where it will always be."

I dragged a finger along the tiny fingertips.

"You were only five when we did that," he said. "You had the cutest little hands then. Your mother and I used to kiss your fingertips before we tucked you in at night."

"Yeah?"

He nodded. "You'd always pretend we missed one and make us start over."

I laughed.

"It's amazing you're so well adjusted considering how hard we tried to spoil you."

"Thanks, Dad. I try."

"Jolie."

I raised my eyebrows.

"Someday when it's time for you to settle down with someone- when it's time for you to start a family of your own- promise me you'll choose a man who loves every single part of you. Even the parts you're not proud of. "

I swallowed.

"Right down to your fingertips."

"I can't promise I'm going to meet someone like that, Dad."

"I know," he said. "But any man who doesn't fit that description is an idiot who doesn't deserve you."

"Okay."

"Don't forget," he said, tapping his forehead.

"I won't," I promised.

And I never did.

THIRTY SEVEN
- Jolie -

I'd never been so sick.

I couldn't think straight, couldn't swallow. My appetite was wonky and my fuse was shorter than normal.

Sleep had become as elusive as Bigfoot, and I'd grown physically clumsy in a way that made it hard to recognize myself.

It was only when I began searching my symptoms online that I got any clarity at all.

As I typed my extensive list of qualms into the search bar, my mind wandered to how quickly my brain tumor might take over. Then, just before I pressed search, my eye caught the last symptom I'd typed.

I can't stop thinking about him.

Fuck. Suddenly I was wishing for that tumor.

I hit enter and waited.

Perhaps not surprisingly, the first result that came up was an article about how love makes you sick. I read it twice, finding myself particularly horrified by the assertion that its effect on the body was similar to the feelings one got from smoking crack.

This seemed odd, though, since smoking crack was supposed to make you feel awesome and I felt dreadful.

On the other hand, I kind of understood the addiction part of it because no matter how much the symptoms escalated, I kept wanting the thing that made me feel so shitty in the first place.

Adam Darling: the only guy I'd ever really wanted and the only guy whose wanting me ever made me feel alive.

By the time I read the article three times, I was convinced I'd developed the chest pains it alluded to.

And then it dawned on me. My illness seemed to be worsening in direct correlation to how much effort I was putting into avoiding him, which was a lot.

I'd stopped taking his calls outside of office hours, stopped discussing business with him in private, insisting we meet in public places. And even when we did meet, I avoided making eye contact with him as much as possible so he wouldn't see the truth in my eyes.

So he wouldn't see that I did love him back.

So he didn't see that it was killing me.

But I knew it was stupid. I mean, what kind of person realizes they're in love with someone after they break things off?

Still, there was no denying it. Of course I was in love with him.

How could I not be? He was Prince Charming and I was Cinderella.

Except there was no ball, no slipper, no friendly band of talking mice. And all those things were as unlikely as us ending up together.

We were from different worlds, and it was naïve to think I could change his mind and make him love me enough to stay here when he'd never done anything but entertain me for the summer and fuck off.

Therefore, I had to keep reminding myself how much worse the pain would be if I allowed myself to fall any harder.

Fortunately I hadn't already told him I loved him, which was the only thing keeping me strong and making me feel half convincing.

And while I knew love wasn't the kind of thing you were supposed to extinguish in your own fist, I'd buried that secret as deep inside me as I could- so deep that if I were a squirrel I'd never find it again, and it would dissolve in the Earth under countless winter frosts.

A text alert jolted me from my pessimistic spiral of self-loathing, reminding me that there was a staff meeting in five minutes.

I made sure all the room service orders were being prepared and that no one was due to check out in the next half hour. Then I made my way to the conference room.

In the last week and a half, the room had been redone from top to bottom, and the delicious smell of fresh paint lingered faintly in the air.

I looked around for Gia, whose wet hair was pulled back in a claw, and made my way over to her.

"Hey," she said. "Any idea what this is about?"

I shrugged. "I wouldn't be surprised if it was just a meeting for discussing future meetings."

"Or a meeting to discuss how much nicer the meeting room is now?"

I nodded.

Her eyes smiled as she folded her arms and turned towards the voice clearing at the front of the room.

I watched Adam stand up at the front of the room, his day old stubble making his face look even more chiseled than usual. I recalled how it felt to have him drag it up my neck, which gave me such a visible chill Gia glanced over her shoulder at me.

"Thanks for being punctual everybody," he said, clasping his hands in front of him. "I won't take much of your time as I don't want you all high on paint fumes for the rest of the day."

A few guys from the kitchen laughed too loud.

"But I do have two important announcements to make," he said, standing with his feet shoulder width apart. "Unfortunately, it's sort of a good news/bad news situation."

I raised my eyebrows, a feeling of horror sweeping through me. Surely he would discuss bad news with me in private before mentioning it to the rest of the staff?

"I'll start with the good news," he said. "Which is that we've had a lucky break."

Everyone in the room leaned towards him.

"In light of the changes we've made at the hotel recently, a high profile friend of mine has decided he'd like to get married here. His fiancée happens to be even more famous than he is, however, so I can't divulge who the happy couple is out of respect for their security requirements."

I furrowed my brows.

Gia turned around and raised hers at me.

"However, you can rest assured that the event is sure to create some fantastic buzz about the place in the media, and it couldn't be a better time for us to get some publicity. Best of all, because the event is going to require additional work from all of you- as well as a lot of discretion- you're all going to be incentivized for putting in the extra time and effort."

Someone whistled at the back of the room, triggering a round of applause.

"Who is it?" someone shouted. "Who's the couple?"

"I've been sworn to secrecy," he said. "But you'll all find out soon enough."

"Is that the bad news?" someone asked. "That you can't tell us who it is?"

Adam clenched his jaw and took a deep breath. "No. The bad news is of a more personal nature."

I held my breath as the room went quiet.

"The bad news is that I'm only going to stay until the end of the summer," he said.

I froze.

"I'm keen to see the renovations through," he continued. "And I've promised to see to it that the wedding is a success, but I won't be staying on at Harmony Bay."

I hugged myself as a hand went up near the front of the room.

"Why?" the woman asked. "We thought you liked it here?"

"I do like it here," he said, his eyes scanning the room. "Very much. And I've enjoyed getting to know all of you."

"So what's the problem?" the woman asked.

"I've fallen in love," he said.

My stomach dropped.

"With Jolie Monroe."

My lips fell apart.

Everyone in the room turned to look at me.

"Those of you that know her well will understand why," he said. "But regrettably, the situation has compromised my ability to be professional in this role."

I swallowed.

"And even more disappointing-" His eyes found mine. "She doesn't love me back."

I pressed my lips together.

"And I know it will prove too painful for me to work closely with her long term."

This isn't happening. This isn't happening. This isn't happening.

I broke his gaze and stared down at my feet, hoping they'd be wearing not glass, but sequined ruby slippers.

They weren't.

"That being said," Adam continued. "I'm more determined than ever to make every day count here, and I look forward to finalizing the improvements that will make this the finest resort in the Outer Banks."

I lifted my eyes in time to see him dismiss everyone, and despite the fact that Gia started talking to me right away, her words were as incomprehensible as if she were underwater.

And for a few minutes, I was sure I was drowning.

Because everything was blurry, and I couldn't tell which way was up.

THIRTY EIGHT
- Adam -

I watched Jolie walk up the driveway from her mother's front room and saw her expression change as she recognized my car.

Then I took a seat at the kitchen table beside my half-drunk tea.

The screen door opened behind me a moment later. "What are you doing here?" she asked, her tone equal parts startled and accusatory.

I turned to look over my shoulder. "We need to talk."

She scoffed. "I'll say. What the hell were you thinking?"

"Jolie!" Her mom laid her hands on the butcher block. "Since when do you speak to guests this way?"

"Sorry- did you say guest?" she asked, craning her neck forward. "I think you mean pest."

Her mom parted her lips to object, but I raised a hand faster. "It's okay, Mrs. Monroe. I knew Jolie would be angry with me when I showed up here. I should've warned you."

She furrowed her brows. "Angry? Whatever for?"

I sighed. "I admitted to the entire staff that I was in love with her earlier today. Unfortunately, she didn't take it as well as they did."

"They didn't take it well either," Jolie said. "And you didn't need to share that information with my mother on top of everything."

Mrs. Monroe cocked her head. "I'm not sure I understand what's going on."

"Me neither," Jolie said, folding her arms.

"I came for your signature," I said, pulling a folded stack of papers from the inside pocket of my sports coat.

She squinted at me. "Because...?"

"Because I can't sign the hotel over to you unless I have your written permission," I said, setting the papers on the table.

"Sign it over to her?" her mom asked. "But you just bought it?"

"And now I want to give it away," I said. "To Jolie."

Jolie turned an ear towards me. "For nothing?"

I shook my head. "Not for nothing."

"I don't get what's in it for you," Jolie said, leaning against the butcher block.

"Some time with you is all I was after," I said. "And if it's going to come to nothing as you say, I should respect your wishes and be on my way."

She dropped her head for a moment. "You don't have to do this."

"Oh but I do."

"I'll leave you two alone," her mom said, inching towards the front room. "It sounds like you have some things to discuss."

"Don't worry about it, Mom. We'll go upstairs."

I raised my eyebrows.

"You can bring your tea," Jolie said before walking out the door and stomping up the worn grey steps.

"You're in love with her?" Mrs. Monroe asked me in a hushed voice.

"I am," I said, slipping the papers back in my pocket.

"Why does she seem so angry about it?" she asked, still whispering.

"Hopefully I can figure that out," I said, rising to my feet.

She nodded. "Good luck."

I thanked Mrs. Monroe, walked up the back steps, and knocked on the edge of the screen door.

Jolie threw it open and gave me an exasperated look. "What are you trying to do, Adam?"

"Drive you crazy?" I joked, stepping inside.

The lofted space was surprisingly open, and while she'd obviously tried to make some sort of visible separation between the sitting room and the bedroom, they were one and the same.

"I'll say," she said, pulling a bottle of vodka out of the freezer and making herself a short screwdriver.

"For what it's worth, there are other ways I prefer to do it," I said, my eyes lingering on her unmade bed.

"I can't buy the hotel from you, and you know it."

"I'm not asking you to buy it," I said. "But you're the rightful owner and the only one I trust to make sure my investment doesn't go to waste."

"So that's it?" she asked. "You're just going to fuck off because I hurt your feelings?"

I walked up to her, backing her into the corner of her kitchen. "You didn't hurt my feelings, Jolie." Her lips were so close to mine all I could think about was tasting them. "You broke my fucking heart."

Her eyes bounced between mine.

"There's a big difference."

"Don't you think you're exaggerating?" she asked.

"Don't you think you should sign the papers and stop torturing me?" I pulled them from inside my jacket and held them in the narrow space between us. "The sooner I can start making arrangements to leave, the sooner I can look forward to getting over you."

"I'm not the only one who cares about you here," she said, pushing past me. "No one else wants you to leave."

"But you don't want me to stay."

She pushed a hand up her forehead. "I didn't say that."

I tossed the folded papers on the world's smallest kitchen table. "Ever since you told me off, you've done nothing but made me feel unwelcome here. Why should I put up with that?"

"I'm sorry. I'm not trying to make you uncomfortable. I'm just trying to keep from getting hurt."

I furrowed my brow. "By hurting me?"

"What am I supposed to do?"

"You're supposed to let me love you," I said. "And you're supposed to love me back."

"But I don't." She swallowed. "And I never will."

It hurt to hear her say it again. And I swear the more she said it, the more I feared that I would start to believe it. "Then I can't stay."

She took a deep breath and lifted the folded stack of papers off the table.

I watched her eyes scan the first page.

I lowered my voice. "I wouldn't hurt you, you know?"

She turned the page and kept reading.

"I understand a woman's inclination to protect herself, but you don't have to protect yourself from me."

"Look," she said, lifting her eyes. "I care about you, Adam. I do. You must know that."

"I'm listening."

"But I know all about your intentions, and I know how this story is going to end."

I shook my head. "What are you talking about?"

"Your mom told me everything."

"What?"

"She explained the situation perfectly, and I get why you picked up with me again. I do. And I understand why you'd want a bit of a release this summer with all the stress of work getting on you, but I want you to move on."

I narrowed my eyes at her.

"I want you to have fun with someone who isn't going to be as hurt as I'll be when you leave at the end of the summer."

I stepped up to her.

"I'm sure there's no shortage of girls who want to be used by you, but I'm not one of them," she said. "And I don't have it in me to use you back. We have too much history, too much… chemistry."

I put my hands on her shoulders. "Jolie."

She looked at me, her brown eyes pleading like a tired puppy's. "What?"

"I have no idea what the hell you're talking about."

THIRTY NINE
- Jolie -

My heart was pounding. Why did I have to open my big mouth?

Adam pulled out one of my kitchen chairs. "Sit down."

I let his hand nudge me towards the seat.

He grabbed the other chair and pulled it up beside me. "I want you to think very carefully for a second."

"I haven't been very good at that lately."

"I'm serious," he said without blinking. "I need you to tell me exactly what my mother said to you."

"I'm not sure I remember."

"Jolie, please." He sat back. "It's important."

I stared at him until I realized I had nothing to lose by telling the truth. "She said you don't really love me." I glanced down at my lap. "The same way you don't love Victoria."

He clenched his fist and splayed it out against his thigh. "What else?"

"She said you were going to break up with me at the end of the summer." As hard as it was to repeat her words out loud, something about letting them out made me feel lighter. "She said you were just looking for a good time, and that she wanted to warn me so I wouldn't get hurt."

His lips twitched and the corners of his eyes sagged in a way I'd never seen. "Is there anything else?"

"She said it was her dying wish for you to end up with someone like Victoria, someone well-traveled. And educated." I guess I did remember.

He turned away from me, put his elbows on the table, and held his face in his hands.

I waited for a minute, unsure of what to do. "Adam?"

His eyes were glassy when he sat back up, as if he'd been blinking back tears.

"Are you okay?"

He cleared his throat. "I am so sorry."

He looked so hurt I wanted to hug him, but I didn't know if he wanted me to let on that I could see he was upset.

He pushed some hair behind my ear and held one hand against my cheek. "She had no right to say any of those things. They're not even true."

I raised my eyebrows.

"Except for the fact that I don't love Victoria," he said. "And the part about her dying wish."

I bit the inside of my cheek.

"Do you think I could have some of that vodka?" he asked.

I nodded and went to get my glass and an extra before making a quick return trip to grab the orange juice and the vodka.

He poured a shot into his glass and knocked it back, skipping the orange juice entirely.

I watched his mouth pucker as he exhaled sharply.

"That's not bad out of the freezer," he said.

"It's undrinkable if you don't keep it cold."

He topped up my screwdriver before making one for himself.

I scrunched my face. "Do you want to tell me what you're thinking?"

"I do," he said, nodding. "Assuming you're absolutely positive my mom said that shit to you."

"She did."

He sighed. "I wish I could blame it on her being sick, but just because someone has cancer doesn't make them cancerous."

I draped my fingers around the bottom of my glass.

"Bitter," he said. "That's what I mean."

I took a sip of my drink.

"Is this why you've been acting so crazy?" he asked. "Why you've been pushing me away so hard?"

"Can you blame me?"

He squeezed his temples with the hand that wasn't squeezing his drink.

"Do you have a different story you want to tell me?" I asked.

"I don't have any stories," he said. "I only have the truth, and I've been doing nothing but telling you that since I showed up here."

"Wait. So in the suite when you said you loved me...?"

He fixed his eyes on me.

"And in the meeting earlier...?"

"That was the truth," he said. "It's been the truth from the beginning."

I took a deep breath. Part of me wanted to say I loved him, too, but I didn't know if it was a good idea. After all, the hotel papers were still lying between us, and he'd already told everyone he was leaving.

He pulled his phone out of his jacket pocket and laid it on the table. "I was horrified at the way she spoke to you when we got back from our date, like you were some lowly baggage handler that didn't deserve her respect."

I swallowed.

"I told her I was going to put her on the next plane-just like I did with Victoria- if she didn't apologize to you personally."

I remembered the way she avoided shaking my hand that night and felt a burning sensation in my chest. I washed it down with another sip of vodka.

"All that other stuff is made up." He stared at the phone. "Please forget she said any of that. Leaving you is the last thing I want to do."

"But today you said-"

"Because you've given me no choice," he said, lifting his eyes. "And I'm too proud to stick around here while you go on not returning my feelings."

I scooted to the edge of my chair.

"You're not here," he said, picking up his phone and swiping the screen with his thumb.

I watched him hold it up to his ear.

When it started ringing, he put it on speaker.

"What are you doing?" I mouthed.

He raised a finger in front of his lips.

"Hello, honey." His mom's familiar voice rose in the air between us.

He kept his eyes on me. "I have a question for you, Mom."

"I'll do my best to have an answer," she said.

I leaned back in my chair and hugged myself.

"Remember when you were down here visiting? Remember how I told you that I was in love with Jolie?"

"I do."

My heart floated up in my chest.

"Then why the hell would you tell her I didn't love her?" he asked, raising his voice at the black screen. "And that I was going to break up with her at the end of the summer?"

Silence.

"Hello?" he said, craning his neck forward.

"I don't think those were my exact words," she said halfheartedly.

"You fucked up, Mom."

"Oh don't be angry with me, Ad-"

"I'm way past angry," he said.

"I only want the best for you."

"She's the best for me," he said. "And if you're too selfish to see that then... then I don't know if I want you to be part of my life anymore."

"Honey, please," she said. "Forgive me."

He shook his head. "I don't know if I can."

I'd never seen him look so angry.

"I didn't mean to cause any trouble, Adam. I only meant-"

"I don't want to hear it," he said. "I'm only calling to tell you that I know what you did, and that I've never been more disappointed in anyone in my whole life."

"I'm sorry," she said, her voice meek.

He sighed. "If I decide to forgive you, I'll let you know."

I watched him end the call and hang his head. I couldn't tell what he regretted more- the way he'd spoken to her or the things she'd said to me.

"Forgive me," he said. "I never should've left you alone with her."

"Look on the bright side," I said. "Now you don't have to sign the hotel over to me."

He drained his glass. "I want to do that anyway."

"But-"

"If you don't want it, I'll find someone who does."

I gripped the seat of my chair. "Are you sure this is what you want?"

"I'm sure."

I didn't know how to cheer him up. "Well at least you don't have to leave at the end of the summer now."

"No," he said, standing up. "I suppose I don't." He walked his glass over to the sink. "But it's too late now. I've made the announcement and the arrangements, and a man is only as good as his word."

"Can we at least talk about it?" I asked, rising to my feet. "You must have options."

He walked around me and pushed the screen door open. "Have a look over the papers and get them back to me when you can."

"One more drink, Adam. Stay for one more-"

But he was gone before I could finish, and I was left talking to the screen door, feeling more confused than ever.

FORTY
- Adam -

"You wanted to see me?"

I looked up to see Jolie's face peeking into my office. "Hi."

She smiled, timidly. It was the same smile she'd been offering me since we spoke at her place, and I had to admit, I'd been feeling a little out of sorts since then, too.

"What's up?' she asked, taking a seat in the chair opposite my desk. Her long hair was pulled back in a high ponytail that filled my mind with unprofessional thoughts.

"I got the papers you signed back from the lawyer." I slid a manila folder out from under a legal pad I'd been writing on.

"Wow," she said. "He took almost as long with them as I did."

I handed the folder across the desk and watched as she opened it, her glossy lips moving as she scanned the page.

"It's official," I said. "She's all yours."

She looked up at me. "I'm not going to ask if you're sure this is what you wanted because-"

"You already did that six thousand times?"

"Thanking you seems grossly inadequate," she said. "I mean, this is a dream come true for me and my family."

"I know," I said. "I'm just sorry your dad isn't here to congratulate you. I know he'd be really proud."

"I don't know," she said, closing the folder. "It's not like I earned it."

"Yes you did." I folded my hands on the desk. "You've been earning it every day since you started working here, which was...?"

"I think I got my first paycheck when I was seven," she said, smiling at the memory. "For combing the path to the beach all summer."

"That's hard work for a seven year old."

"Tell me about it," she said. "It used to take me all day to do what the landscaping guys do in ten minutes now. I used to worry I was going to turn into Hulk Hogan."

I laughed.

"Thanks, though," she said, lifting the folder. "It means a lot to keep it in the family."

"You would've gotten it back eventually," I said. "Regardless of who took over. And the place is better for it."

She shrugged. "Time will tell."

"Consider it a lucky break and don't look back."

She cast her eyes down at her lap.

"How are things going with the wedding planning?" I asked.

Jolie lit up.

"I didn't call you in here to tell you who the couple is so you can stop making that face."

She groaned. "It's literally killing me. The rumors going around are out of this world."

"I'm aware."

"There are almost as many people speculating about it as there are telling me I'm crazy to let you get away."

I froze. It was the first mention of our relationship she'd made in weeks.

"Your announcement didn't make it easy on me anyway," she said, blushing.

I decided that ignoring the comment was the only thing to do. "Carrie told me you were struggling with the planning in the beginning, but she said you've really come into your own."

Her eyes turned down at the corners when she realized I wasn't interested in talking about us. "She gave me some great tips."

I raised my eyebrows. "Oh?"

"I hope they're great anyway," she said. "I guess we'll find out when the happy couple arrives."

"What did she say?"

"She said I should plan it with the same attention to detail that I would plan my own wedding, except I should actually enjoy it because I'm not the bride."

I nodded.

"And of course she's given me some pointers on little details that will make the whole thing more high end."

"Good," I said. "I'll let her know we're going to keep her on the payroll then."

"Definitely. That girl is worth her weight in gold."

"Let's keep that between us," I said. "We can't afford to pay her any more than we already are."

"Are you still planning on leaving after the wedding?" she asked.

"I am. No sense in hanging around and breathing down your neck when I've done all I can do." God what I wouldn't have given to be breathing down her neck at that moment.

"Can I be honest with you?" she asked, clasping her hands in her lap.

"Of course."

"I've missed you."

A lump formed in my throat.

"I thought we might spend some time together after the misunderstanding with your mom blew over, but you've been so distant."

I leaned back in my chair. "I've just been busy putting the final touches on the renovations so I don't leave you with any loose ends. It's nothing personal."

"So you haven't been staying busy just to keep your mind off me?"

That too. "Of course not."

"I wish I'd never told you to leave, you know?" She held the back of her neck. "I wish I could take it back- all those things I said about not wanting you here."

"Thanks, Jolie. That means a lot to me."

Her shoulders drooped.

"And I agree it would be nice to spend some time together before I leave."

She straightened up in her chair.

"What do you think?" I asked. "One more date? For old times' sake?"

She nodded. "I'd like that."

"Great. My friend already offered to let me take his boat out one last time, and there's no one I'd rather enjoy a sunset with."

"Sounds like a plan," she said. "When did you have in mind?"

"How about Saturday?"

"Perfect."

"I'll pick you up," I said.

"Can I bring something this time?"

"Just yourself," I said. "I'll take care of everything else."

FORTY ONE
- Jolie -

I couldn't believe this was going to be our last date.
The thought was so upsetting I almost chickened out entirely.

But of course I had to come. I knew in my bones I would never care for someone the way I cared for Adam, so I wasn't about to skip the time with him.

His charm delighted me, his physicality turned me on, and seeing the respect he'd shown the hotel and the staff since the beginning of the summer had made me fall for him in more ways than I ever thought possible.

Obviously I wished I could make him change his mind about leaving, but he was even more hard headed than I was, and I had only myself to blame for driving him away, for hurting him in a way I couldn't undo.

If only I hadn't looked him in the eyes and told him I would never love him back.

I didn't even know anymore why I did it. Perhaps I was scared. Perhaps I was out of my depth and afraid of what the future might've held if I'd put myself out there.

But looking back it was a risk I wished I'd taken. Because imagining my life without him these last few weeks made me realize that there are worse mistakes than taking a chance on love.

I was grateful for the gentle breeze that night, which encouraged my worries not to linger too long and made my white maxi dress flutter just the right amount.

I paired it with some silver bangles and some dangly seahorse earrings in the hope that Adam's mind might stray to what was underneath my dress.

And just in case it did, I'd shaved all the way up my thighs and exfoliated every inch of myself… partly out of nervousness and partly in the hope that it would come to something.

After all, I was beginning to think I'd be lucky to get even one more night with him, one more chance to burn myself into his memory, and though I knew better than to hope for it, one more chance to win him back.

He was looking delectably tan in a crisp white button up, and he rolled up the sleeves as soon as it was time to set sail.

I stayed at the stern with him while we made our way out of the marina, watching the muscles in his back shift under his shirt as he steered us out towards the open water.

From time to time, I let my eyes drop to his butt and found myself wishing it were mine to bite and drum on and squeeze playfully.

"Care to pour some drinks?" he asked over his shoulder, his dark hair blowing in the breeze like he was filming a cologne commercial.

"It would be my pleasure," I said, rolling the cooler towards me. "What would you like?"

"Just a beer," he said. "But feel free to open the white for yourself."

"I might start with a beer, too," I said, pulling two bottles from the ice and wondering what it would be like for him to drag a piece of it over me, leaving a trail of cold liquid down to my-

I shook the thought from my mind, popped the caps off, and brought him a beer.

"Thanks," he said, clinking the neck of his beer against mine. "What was it you said the first time we came out?"

I raised my eyebrows. "To old friends and new beginnings?"

He nodded and took a sip.

I looked ahead to the horizon where a medley of bright colors looked like they were warming the sky.

"You want to take the wheel for a second?" he asked.

"Seriously?"

"Of course." He reached for my beer and set it in the closest holder. Then he stepped back to make room for me at the helm.

I gripped the large wooden wheel, which was polished to a high sheen and looked as delicate as the wheel of a racing bike. "Is this right?"

He stepped behind me and slid my hands up each side. "Let's go with ten and two until you get comfortable."

I nodded and tried to breathe normally but it was hard with his body up against mine. He was so close there was no doubt he could smell my hair- maybe even see the goosebumps that erupted on my arms when he put his hands on mine.

"You're a natural," he said, his voice steady and low.

"If anything, it's a little easier than driving my car."

He laughed.

"Seriously. There's no traffic, I'm not trying to navigate through a dirty windshield, and I don't have to worry about coming to any stoplights."

"Actually that makes sense," he said, stepping to the side and letting his hand graze my lower back for a few seconds less than I would've liked. "People are always saying the Nissan Micra is a natural stepping stone to a giant sailboat."

I shot him a look.

He smiled, and my heart melted a little.

"Thanks for bringing me out again," I said, training my eyes back on the horizon. "I could get used to this."

"Which?" he asked. "The sailing or my company?"

"Both."

He reached for his beer and took a swig.

"You know I've known you longer than I've known almost anyone else," I said, wondering how I could make him see how important he was to me without begging him to stay. Not that I was above begging, but I didn't want him to stay out of guilt.

"Besides everyone who works at the hotel you mean?"

"That's different," I said.

He raised his thick eyebrows.

"They're family."

"So I've come to learn," he said. "It was a nightmare trying to figure out who was related to who in the beginning."

"I think that's a testament to my dad," I said. "For building a place that could employ multiple generations."

"Couldn't agree more," he said, lifting my beer towards me.

"You think I'm ready to steer with one hand?"

"I think you can handle it long enough to take a sip."

I gulped two healthy swigs and handed the bottle back to him. "Thanks," I said, licking my lips as I noticed his shirt was unbuttoned one more than I detected earlier.

He caught me looking but didn't call me out. "It's a great group anyway. I had a lot of fun getting to know everyone."

"They certainly enjoyed getting to know you, too," I said. "Though the frequency with which you call staff meetings has become a bit of an inside joke."

His expression fell. "What?"

"Just saying," I said. "I mean, haven't you ever heard of a memo?"

"Are you kidding?" he asked. "Memos are so much worse. Then you have to go around asking people if they got their memos and then you're just a parody of a boss. Not to mention the time suck."

I pressed my lips together to suppress a smile.

"Plus, meetings are better because you can actually see people's faces when you give them news, which means you can tell if they have questions and make sure your announcements don't become a messy game of telephone."

"I suppose you have a point," I said. "Maybe I'll keep it up once you're gone."

"How would you do it?" he asked.

"Well, I used to have a point person in every department, and I'd just inform those people and let them spread the word."

He narrowed his eyes at me.

"It was pretty efficient."

"Maybe," he said. "But that sounds dangerously close to playing favorites, which can be a tricky move when it comes to family."

I cocked my head. "True."

"Besides, I was the new guy, and I wanted people to know me."

"I'm only teasing you," I said. "Your meeting thing obviously worked. You settled in much faster than I anticipated."

"It made me feel comfortable anyway."

"And it was cool that you treated everyone as equals from day one."

"Except for you," he said.

I stole a glance at him.

"Giving you special treatment has been my favorite job of all."

FORTY TWO
- Adam -

"It's funny how similar the view is when the inside has changed so much," Jolie said as we watched the sun set behind the resort.

"Are you happy with the changes?" I asked.

"Are you kidding? The place went from three and a half to five stars. Even the staff has been transformed."

I leaned back and put my arm on the edge of the boat behind her. "Everyone was so devoted to the success of the place. It was a pleasure to be part of it."

She turned and looked at me. "We couldn't have done it without you, you know?"

"You mean you couldn't have done it without Carrie."

"Her, too," Jolie said. "But even bringing her in was your idea."

"True," I said. "I suppose I can take credit for that."

"I can't wait for the wedding, too. Everyone is so excited."

"I'm sure it will be a big success."

She elbowed me in the ribs. "That was your cue to tell me who it's for."

"Can't. I've been sworn to secrecy."

Her lower lip slid out in a pout. "What about my special treatment?"

"What about just taking things as they come?"

She groaned. "You sound like my dad."

"I'll take that as a compliment."

She sighed and scooted a little closer to me.

It felt great to have her so close, but it still didn't feel close enough.

"Do you get sunsets like this in New York?" she asked.

I shook my head. "No. You don't get sunsets like this anywhere."

She raised an eyebrow. "I suppose you've seen a few?"

"I have, yeah."

"Which ones have been the best?"

I kept my eyes on the deep pink swirls glowing over the hotel. "The ones I've seen with you."

"I find that hard to believe."

I turned my head towards her. "Why?"

"Because you've seen so many all over the world."

"I suppose it depends on what you want from a sunset."

"Surely everyone wants the same things from a sunset," she said. "Bright swirls of color, a clear view of the sun, and for the whole sky to be lit up as far as the eye can see."

"All those things are great," I said, breathing in the fresh sea air. "But they pale in comparison to what I want from a sunset."

"Which is what?" she asked, angling her body towards me.

"To see it reflected in the eyes of the woman I love."

Her brown eyes bounced back and forth between mine.

"I still love you, Jolie." I put a hand on her knee. "I know I haven't said it in a while, but I'm still bat shit crazy in love with you."

She lifted my hand off her knee and held it in her hands. "I love you, too, Adam."

My eyes crinkled at the corners.

"I don't know why it's been so hard for me to say it," she said. "Especially when you've been so honest with me from the beginning. But I'd rather tell you before you leave than have you go and not know how much-"

I leaned down and kissed her, and the eagerness with which she opened her mouth to me filled me with fire. Then I lifted her legs across my lap so I could pull her closer as I stirred her sweet tongue in my mouth.

It was the kiss I'd wanted for as long as I could remember, the kiss that meant I'd finally won her heart.

"Thank you," I said, dragging my fingers across her cheek. "You have no idea what it means to me to hear you say that."

She glanced down, her eyelashes casting shadows on her cheeks as the starry night sky crept up from the East. When she looked up again, she laid a hand on my cheek.

I grabbed her wrist and brought her hand between us, kissing her fingertips as I kept my eyes on her, a hunger growing in my belly that I knew would have to be sated soon.

"I wish we could just stay here forever," she whispered, curling her fingers around my hand.

"If I'd known you were going to feel that way, I would've brought more food."

She laughed.

"Unfortunately, with the provisions we've got, we'll be hungry by morning."

"So no sleepovers on the boat tonight?" she asked, her big eyes full of hope.

"I'm afraid not, but we don't have to head back just yet."

"Good," she said.

"Besides, I have a surprise for you."

"A surprise?"

"Consider it a going away present."

"Oh," she said, her tone falling flat. "Okay."

"Give me one second to get it ready," I said, lifting her legs off me. "Then come below deck when I call you."

"Sure."

I made my way to the back of the boat and went down the staircase below deck. Once there, it took me a minute to situate her present in the lounge area, and although I spent the whole time wishing I'd thought to give her something less physically awkward, it was too late now.

Then I made some preparations in the bedroom in case everything went according to plan.

"Ready?" she called from the top of the stairs.

"One second!" I pulled the curtain across the bedroom area and took a deep breath. "Okay, ready."

Jolie's long dress fell from step to step as she descended the stairs, and as soon as she caught sight of the enormous gift, her eyes sprang into tiny crescents.

"What could that be?" she asked.

"Have a guess," I said, turning my palms up.

"Well, it's shaped a lot like a paddle board," she said, her eyes scanning the wrapped package that stretched across the floor between us. "But you could be trying to throw me off."

I rocked back on my heels, trying to control my anticipation.

"I didn't even know they made bows that big," she said, nodding at the oversized red bow.

I nodded. "You can get anything on Amazon these days."

"Good to know."

"Open it already!" I said, waving my hands at the package.

She tilted her head. "But then the moment will be over."

I groaned. "Maybe the next moment will be even better. Did you ever think of that?"

She lifted her dress, dropped to her knees, and pulled one of the ribbons sticking out of the bow. It unraveled instantly, and she glanced up at me before turning her focus to the shiny wrapping paper. "Looks like a paddle board alright," she said, tearing away.

Suddenly, the message written across the board in bold cursive became visible.

She only stared at the words "Will You Marry Me" for a moment before looking up.

"Would you mind standing again for this next part?" I asked, extending a hand.

She let me help her to her feet, her eyes on mine as the flush disappeared from her cheeks.

That's when I took a knee in the middle of the paddle board and pulled a small box out of my back pocket. "Jolie-"

Her mouth fell open.

"Ever since the day I met you, you've been teaching me, testing me, and turning me on." I took a deep breath. "I feel like I've spent my whole life trying to get back to you."

She put a hand over her chest.

"And I don't want to enjoy another breakfast, another day at the beach, or another sunset without you."

She batted her eyelashes and pressed her lips together.

"For years, I've been trying to figure out what I want, and it turns out it's been you all along. You and you alone." I clenched my jaw and willed my voice not to shake. "I love every beautiful inch of you, and I always will. Because you're my soulmate. And I want to spend the rest of my life making sure that gorgeous smile never leaves your face." I popped the ring box open. "Marry me so I never have to say goodbye to you again."

Her eyes filled with tears and she sank to her knees. "Of course I'll marry you," she said, throwing her arms around me. "Despite how horribly cruel you were to let me think you were going to leave me again!"

"Never," I said, pulling her tight, my whole body flooding with warmth.

She sat back on her heels and wiped her eyes as she shook her head at me. "I can't believe how good you duped me."

I pulled the ring from the box and took her hand. "But it's all okay now, right? Since you're the only person I want to dupe?"

She nodded.

So I slid the ring on her finger.

FORTY THREE
- Jolie -

I held my hand out and looked at the diamond ring, but as stunning as it was, it wasn't enough to distract me from Adam's beaming face.

"You like it?" he asked.

I nodded.

"Amazon again. Go figure."

I laughed and pushed his chest, which didn't even budge.

"I'm joking," he said.

"I know," I said, glancing at the sparkling ring again.

He raised his brows. "Happy?"

"I would've been happy with the paddle board."

"You know what I mean."

"I do," I said. "The only thing that worries me is that I don't know if I said yes because I'm bat shit crazy about you, too, or because I would do anything to keep you from leaving."

"What's the difference?" he asked.

"Good point."

"Also, that's not funny."

I laughed. "Oh, so you can dish it out, but you can't take it. Is that it?"

"Oh I can take it," he said, smiling as he crawled over me. "I just like it better when you do."

"Me too," I said, trailing a finger down the open part of his shirt.

"Now for another less delicate- but no less important-question."

"Shoot," I said, pulling his belt strap through the buckle.

"Do you want me to have you on your new paddle board, or would you rather I escort you to the bedroom?"

I tilted my head. "That's a tough decision."

"If it helps, I covered the bed with rose petals," he said, dragging my dress up my legs with one hand.

"You were that confident I was going to say yes, huh?"

"Frankly, I did everything I could to ignore any other possibility," he said, sliding his hand between my legs and heating me up with his fingertips. "So what'll it be? The board or the bed?"

"I can't think when you're touching me like that," I said, my breath skipping in my throat.

He slipped his belt from the loops and pulled his shirt off over his head.

My eyes lingered over his rippling abs until he bent back over to kiss me, pulling my underwear off as he did so.

I leaned back as he pushed my dress up around my waist and rubbed between my legs again, his fingers slipping in my silk.

When he dropped his face to my neck and slid his fingers inside me, I gasped, my whole body clenching around him.

"God how I've needed this," he whispered, driving his thick fingers deeper.

His touch felt so good I felt my tear ducts twitch. And as he churned my insides, he kissed his way down to my chest, sliding the straps of my dress and bra off so he could take my puckered nipples in his mouth.

A moment later, he lifted his face, pulled his fingers from me, and sucked them clean before licking his lips.

I raised my eyebrows.

"If I didn't know any better, I'd say you taste just like my fiancée."

A smile spread across my face.

"I know what you're thinking, though," he said, scooting down between my legs. "I better double check to be sure."

I gripped the edge of the board as he made contact, his tongue lapping at my pussy gently at first and then speeding up until my sensitive clit was buzzing.

"I'm gonna come," I panted, pressing my lower back against the board.

"Not without me, you're not," he said, his voice hot between my legs. He wiped his mouth against my inner thigh and sat up. "We do things together from now on."

I watched him unzip his pants, my mouth watering as he pulled his cock out.

He pushed his pants down and took them off without taking his focus off me.

"Take me to bed," I said, licking my lips.

He slid his arms under me, sat back on his heels, and rose to his feet.

I couldn't believe how effortlessly he whisked me through the cabin, and I felt so safe and happy in his arms I thought my heart might burst.

When we reached the thick curtain that separated the bedroom, he nodded, and I pulled it open.

The white bed was covered with dark red rose petals, and there was a champagne bucket on the bedside table.

He stood me up on the end of the low bed so his head was level with my breasts, and he dragged my dress down over my hips until it pooled around my ankles.

Then he slid his hands up the back of my legs and dug his fingertips into the cheeks of my ass like it belonged to him.

I sank down in front of him, taking his cock in my hands as I knelt on the bed.

He stared down at me as I stroked him, and his shaft was so solid in my hand I felt a flash of sexual fear that made me even wetter than I already was.

I lowered my head and took him in my mouth, stroking him with one hand and pulling his ass towards me with the other.

He groaned and leaned into me as I pushed his thick cock to the back of my throat, relishing the sweet taste of his clean skin.

I was lost in sucking him by the time he pulled my hair back and lifted his chin towards the top of the bed.

I read the look in his eyes and scooted back, admiring his naked body as the rose petals kissed my skin.

"And you didn't even want to open the paddle board," he said, a sly smile on his face.

"I want you inside me," I said, suddenly conscious of the gentle waves lapping against the hull.

He crawled over me, his dark eyes full of lust.

"I've wanted you inside me every day since-"

"Shhh." He pressed a finger across my lips. "I know." He grabbed his dick and pressed his head against my slit. "I've wanted you, too," he said, fixing his eyes on mine as he forced me open.

I felt drunk on his attention, on the feel of him throbbing inside me, and on the love I felt for him. It was like I was sloppier than I'd ever been but also like I was seeing everything with more clarity than ever before.

And as he rocked his hips over me, hitting me deep like only he could, I realized the sick tension I'd been feeling for weeks had gone away.

All because he loved me back.

It was a sort of stars aligned feeling I'd never experienced before. And as I pressed my head into the pillow and inhaled the rose petals around me, the man

I loved made love to me, and I knew in my heart that I'd gotten my prince.

Adam lifted up so he could rub my clit, his abs flexing over me with his shallow breathing.

I bit my lip and furrowed my brow. "I'm close."

He sat back and pulled my legs straight up against his chest, holding my thighs as he fucked me with his fingers on my swollen bud.

"Come with me," I said.

He swelled even more as he concentrated on my pleasure, his gaze traveling from my belly button ring to my tits to my lips to my eyes.

Suddenly the pressure was too much, and when my orgasm shattered through me, I grabbed fistfuls of petals as Adam thrust deep inside me one last time, groaning as he filled me with his desire.

We collapsed in a panting mess on the bed, and I wrapped my arms around him, conscious of my engagement ring again only when I laid my hands across his back.

"I fucking love you," he panted against my ear.

I laughed. "I fucking love you, too."

When he caught his breath, he rolled onto his side. "So what did you prefer?" he asked. "The bed or the board?"

"Gee I don't know. It's all such a blur now."

He dragged a finger across my cheek, admiring me in a way that made me feel safe and beautiful.

I rolled towards him and propped the pillow up under my head. "Can I ask you something?"

"Anything."

"Do you think now that I'm your fiancée, you can trust me to keep the secret of whose wedding I've been planning?"

He smiled. "You really want to know, don't you?"

"Desperately."

His dark eyes bounced between mine.

I raised my eyebrows. "Well?"

"Ours."

I lifted my head. "What?"

"You've been planning our wedding."

"But-"

"That's why Carrie told you to plan it like it was your own."

My eyes went wide. "Are you serious?"

He nodded. "As serious as the ring on your finger."

I glanced down at it again as if it were proof that I hadn't imagined the whole thing.

"Surprise."

"Jesus, Adam." I sat up. "Here I was hoping I'd be able to just win you back, and I've been planning our wedding this whole time?!"

"Surprise."

"You said that already."

He rolled onto his back. "That's because I can't tell if you're thrilled or pissed."

"I'm surprised."

"Surprise!"

"Stop that," I said, pointing at him. "I need to think."

"About what?"

"About the fact that I've just agreed to marry a crazy person."

He smiled. "If it makes you feel better, I really feel like I understand."

I pushed his chest. "Don't you get it? I've spared no expense. It's going to be the most over the top, romantic wedding ever."

"I feel so lucky to be invited."

I collapsed back on the pillow, my mind racing with thoughts about whether I chose the right cake, the right band, the right menu.

"Relax, Jo. Everything's done. All you need is a dress."

"What about invitations?"

"I'll call a meeting."

I slapped a hand over my face. "This is crazy."

"You want to know the craziest part of all?" he asked.

I shook my head. "Sure."

"You know how I've been busting everyone's chops so the renovations would be finished before I left?"

"Yeah."

"That's so I can take you on an epic honeymoon without either of us having to worry about the place."

I sprang back up. "An epic honeymoon?!"

He nodded. "Champagne?"

"Yes. Of course. Champagne fifteen minutes ago."

A moment later, there was a large boom, followed by a crackling sound.

I looked up. "What was that?"

"I don't know," he said, sitting up. "Maybe we should go check."

I grabbed my dress from the floor and slipped it on, leaving my underwear where it lay.

"I'll meet you on deck," Adam said, grabbing the champagne bucket.

I reached the top of the stairs just in time to see a huge gold firework go off over the water. "Hurry up!" I called down to him. "It's fireworks!"

He arrived a few booms later wearing a white robe with the champagne bucket and two flutes in hand.

"This is amazing," I said, taking a seat on the cushioned bench at the back of the boat.

Adam sat beside me and popped the cork in time with the next colorful explosion while I kept my eyes on the sky full of blinking stars above.

"Here," Adam said, passing me a glass of champagne. "To the rest of our lives."

I smiled and clinked my glass against his. "Wait a second," I said after I took a sip. "Did you set this up?"

He pointed at the sky. "What? This?"

"You did, didn't you?"

"I might've called in a favor."

"Wow," I said. "You might be crazy, but no one could question your attention to detail."

"Thanks," he said, his chiseled features lit up by the flashing sky.

"You want to tell me what else you've got up those sleeves of yours?"

"Absolutely not," he said, putting his arm around me.

I turned towards him and watched the fireworks sparkle across his eyes as they boomed overhead.

Then he leaned forward and kissed me, the sweet taste of champagne dancing on our tongues as my heart danced in my chest.

And for the first time in my life, I had no idea what tomorrow would bring, but there was one thing I did know, and that was that I'd never been happier.

FORTY FOUR
- Adam -

"I can't believe you're getting married tomorrow," Christophe said, leaning back in his chair. "I want to be happy for you, but you were such a good wingman it kind of feels like a death."

I watched Jolie straighten my godson's bowtie across the room before checking my watch and thinking I should find his mother so our ring bearer wasn't sleeping on the job tomorrow.

"I have to be honest," Ben said. "I definitely thought Carrie and I would beat you to the altar."

"I can't believe she didn't tell you my plan," I said. "I was sure she'd spill the beans."

"I'm as surprised as you are," Ben said, reaching for the champagne in the middle of the round table. "Then again, that woman never ceases to amaze me."

My eyes drifted across the banquet hall before settling on my parents, who were at the bar we'd set up for the occasion.

I was relieved that my mother had come, but I was starting to think it was too much to hope that she would ever accept Jolie into our family the way my dad had so enthusiastically.

"Your dad seems to have taken quite a shine to Jolie," Ben said, loosening his tie.

I nodded. "I think he's genuinely happy for me. Not that I'm surprised by that. The only relationship advice I can ever remember him giving me was to marry someone who made me laugh."

"That's it?" Christophe asked.

"That's it," I said. "He told me everything else goes-money, looks, energy, health- none of it lasts. He said a sense of humor is the only thing that stands any chance of getting better with age."

Christophe squinted at me. "Did he give you that advice before or after he married your mother?"

I raised my eyebrows. "What are you saying?"

"Adam's mom is actually pretty hilarious," Ben said. "It's just that her timing is usually completely inappropriate."

"Has she forgiven you for breaking up with Victoria?" Christophe asked.

I shrugged. "I don't really care. To be honest, I don't give a shit if she punishes me for the rest of my life. I just don't want her to take it out on Jolie."

"Jolie's got thick skin," Ben said. "She can handle herself."

"I know," I said, slinging my arm over the empty chair beside me. "I just feel bad that her entire extended family has welcomed me with open arms, and I can't even get my mother to stop thinking of her as the little girl that used to clear our plates."

Ben furrowed his brow. "She used to clear your plates?"

"Yeah," I said. "She's been working here her whole life."

Ben shook his head. "Damn. Kinda makes me feel a little better about not living with my dad growing up."

Christophe laughed so hard his eyes watered.

"What?" Ben asked.

"The thought of you toiling away in the Abbott," he said. "I just got this mental image of you covered in soot in the basement trying to keep the place warm."

"You're an idiot," Ben said.

"Speaking of idiots-" I drained my whiskey. "I can't thank you guys enough for coming."

"Are you kidding?" Ben asked. "Wouldn't have missed it."

Christophe shrugged. "I didn't have anything else better to do."

I rolled my eyes.

"Seriously, though." Christophe stood up just enough to reach across the table and snatch the champagne from Ben. "Of course I came. This wedding wouldn't even be happening if it weren't for me."

Ben raised his eyebrows. "Come again?"

"I don't know about that," I said. "But you did give me some good advice in the beginning."

"What advice?" Ben asked. "How to get a girl to feel so unwelcome in the morning she'll leave before you have to make her breakfast?"

I laughed.

"How to get a girl to make out with her friend," Ben continued.

"No," Christophe said, his face turning red.

Ben cocked his head. "How to blank an ex when you're with someone new?"

"Enough!" Christophe said. "You don't live with me anymore. Stop acting like you know all my moves."

Ben laughed. "I do know all your moves."

"Actually," I said, feeling like it was time to pull Christophe from under the bus. "The advice he gave me wasn't sleazy at all."

"See," Christophe said, raising his palm towards me.

"Even if there were a few more animal analogies than were really necessary."

Christophe groaned and dropped his head back. "I don't know what I did to deserve such ungrateful friends."

"Hey," I said, leaning forward. "I'm only joking. You saved my ass. I owe you one."

"Then why didn't you make me your best man instead of Ben?" he asked.

Ben raised his eyebrows.

I scrunched my face. "Because I feared that when it came time to do the speeches, I'd have to worry about your taste level."

Ben smiled. "And your animal references."

"This is bullshit," Christophe said. "You guys are assholes."

"Also," I said, "I figured that if I didn't bog you down with unnecessary responsibilities, it would give you more time to get reacquainted with Gia, who- for the record- isn't bringing a plus one."

Christophe's face lifted. "Is that so?"

I nodded.

"Maybe you're not such a bad friend after all," he said.

"Thanks," I said, loosening my tie. "Besides, Ben's going to need the distraction so he doesn't notice how many of the staff here have fallen in love with his wife to be."

"Trust me, I'm aware," he said. "We can't even eat in the restaurant here anymore because she's too buddy buddy with everyone."

I laughed. "They're her biggest fans."

Ben shook his head. "She already told Javier she'd come down and celebrate Cinco de Mayo with his family next year."

I raised my eyebrows. "I guess I'll look forward to seeing you next May."

"Count on it," Ben said, looking around. "I'm never letting her out of my sight again." When he found her, he scrunched his face. "Is that the busboy that proposed to her last week?"

I nodded.

He groaned.

"Relax," I said. "He's just a kid."

"Where did Christophe disappear to?" he asked.

I lifted my chin towards the bar, where he was already propped up beside Gia.

"Damn," Ben said. "She is wearing that dress."

"No shit," I said. "Like she was poured into it. I can see his eyes hanging out from here."

"Gotta admire his energy, though," Ben said. "The guy's an eternal optimist."

"Hey, handsome," Jolie said, sliding a hand onto my shoulder and setting a fresh whiskey down in front of me.

"Please tell me you accept tips," I said, pulling her arm down into the chair beside me.

"Here's a tip," Ben said. "Take him home already."

I narrowed my eyes at him. "Why don't you go check on your own fiancée?"

"Now that's a good tip," he said, topping up his glass and heading across the room.

"How's it going?" Jolie asked, her eyes as sparkly as her earrings.

"Pretty well," I said. "I've got a good buzz going, and I'm going to marry the love of my life tomorrow."

"She must be a special lady to deserve the affection of a man as charming as yourself."

"She is," I said, fixing my eyes on her. "She's everything a man could want and more."

"What's the more?"

My mouth curled into a smile. "I'm hoping she shows me after we say I do."

She blushed. "Challenge accepted."

"And you?" I asked. "You seem like you're in a good mood."

"Of course."

"Care to explain?" I asked.

"It's simple, really," she said. "When I was a little girl, I taught a handsome boy how to fly a kite."

"I remember."

She smiled. "And I've been high ever since."

FORTY FIVE
- Jolie -

I was afraid I wouldn't recognize myself when I put on the dress, but that wasn't the case at all.

Not only did I look like a bride from head to toe, but I felt like one, too, from my white satin shoes to the tips of my French manicure. Best of all, I felt like a bride where it counted most- in my heart.

And while I couldn't stop the thoughts looping through my mind about all the things that could go wrong, there was one thing I wasn't worried about, and that was whether or not he was the right guy.

About that, I sincerely had no doubts.

So as much as I was looking forward to enjoying the day surrounded by our family and friends, it was tomorrow I was looking forward to most, a tomorrow where we would wake up for the first time as husband and wife and start our lives together.

I looked over my shoulder when I heard a knock at the door.

Gia came in a second later and put her large purse down on the bed.

"Well?" I asked, turning around carefully so as not to step on my dress.

She clasped her hands together. "Everything is going according to plan so far."

"Go on."

"Ben and Adam are enjoying mimosas."

My mouth fell open.

"Ours are on their way."

I relaxed my shoulders again.

"There was a minor hiccup with the ring bearer."

I tilted an ear towards her. "Meaning?"

She scrunched her face. "The flower girl pushed him into the pool."

"What? Why were they even anywhere near-"

"Don't worry," she said. "He didn't have the ring on him, and he's going to swap clothes with his brother. Well, not swap because his suit is all wet but-"

"Where's my mom?"

"She said she couldn't come back because she just redid her makeup, and she doesn't want to get emotional again."

"But-"

"Trust me," Gia said. "It's the right call. I told her how beautiful you looked in your dress, and the thought alone was enough to set her off."

"Shit."

"My mom's plowing her with tissues as we speak."

I dropped my head.

"But I have good news, too."

I lifted my head in time to see her pull a mahogany urn out of her purse. "Is that-?"

"Your mom said she was never good with this kind of thing." She plopped the urn down on my makeup table. "But she said your dad would know just what to say."

"Fuck," I said, my voice squeaking. "Now I'm going to cry."

"Don't you dare," she said, raising a finger at me. "We don't have time to redo your face, which is glowing by the way."

I looked up and blinked back the tears.

"And I'm not going to say how much I wish your dad were here to see you now, but-"

"Gia!"

She gave me an awkward hug that would've been nicer if we weren't both so desperately trying to keep our faces from touching anything.

"Hurry up and tell me something happy so my eyes aren't puffy when I go out there," I said, trying not to think about my dad.

"Ben said he's never seen Adam happier."

I smiled. "Really?"

She nodded. "He said the guy's on cloud nine, and that all he's been doing this morning is asking how you are."

"And drinking mimosas."

"Ben said they haven't even gone through a bottle yet."

My eyes popped open. "A bottle?! What the hell? What about us?"

"I told you, ours is coming."

I sighed.

"Also, I slept with Christophe last night."

I flinched. "What?"

"We stayed up all night, and I'm covered in the weirdest hickies ever."

"All night?!"

"Don't worry," she said. "I had three Five Hour Energy's this morning so I'm good until-" She squinted at the ceiling.

"Later?"

"Yeah," she said. "Later."

"Well, I'm glad you had a fun night."

"Like so much fun I can't wear white on my own wedding day now."

I burst out laughing and couldn't stop. It was like the stress had turned to giggles. "Oh my god I can't breathe."

She started laughing, too, and the room was suddenly filled with such a blissful lightness I was convinced someone was pumping laughing gas through the vents.

Fortunately, a knock came a moment later and – confident it was the mimosas- we collected ourselves.

But when Gia pulled the door open, Adam's mom was standing there with her hands folded around the strap of her beaded clutch.

"Mrs. Darling," I said. "Come in."

Gia craned her neck down the hallway and gestured for someone to hurry up.

"Hello, Jolie," Mrs. Darling said as she crossed the room.

Carrie's favorite busboy wheeled in a trolley a moment later, and it was everything I could do to ignore Gia pouring champagne in the background.

"What can I do for you?" I asked, focusing on Adam's mom.

"Nothing at all," she said. "I'm actually here because I'd like to do something for you."

I swallowed.

She reached in her purse and pulled out a diamond and coral brooch.

When I realized it was a seahorse, my lips fell apart.

"I didn't know if you had your something old yet," she said. "But this has been in our family since the nineteenth century, since before we even came to this country."

"It's beautiful."

"Adam told me you liked seahorses."

I nodded. "I have a seahorse tattoo."

She blushed. "He didn't tell me that."

I pressed my lips together.

"Anyway, I have lots of little knickknacks like this."

I couldn't believe I was about to marry someone whose mother would describe a diamond covered antique as a knickknack.

"And stories to go with them," she said.

"I bet."

She handed it to me. "And I'm looking forward to having a daughter to share them with."

"Thanks, Mrs. Darling. That really means a lot."

"You're welcome," she said. "And please call me Annette."

"Sure."

"I thought maybe you could pin it to your bouquet or something."

"That's a great idea," I said, dragging my fingers over the pink coral fins.

"And I want to apologize for the first impression you must have of me," she said. "I was reluctant to give you a chance because I had my own ideas of what I wanted for Adam, but I'm very proud that he's followed his heart."

My eyes smiled.

"Maybe I didn't spoil him too rotten after all."

"No," I said. "I think he turned out pretty well."

"Thank you."

I searched her cloudy eyes.

"Anyway," she continued. "I know he loves you very much, and if you have half as much class as this wedding you've put together, then my family is very lucky to have you."

"I really appreciate that, Annette."

"Care to stay for a mimosa, Mrs. D?" Gia asked.

"No," she said, heading towards the door. "I'll leave you girls to it."

I thanked her again and followed her out.

Gia had a mimosa at the ready as soon as I closed the door. "That was pretty cool."

"Yeah," I said. "It was."

"How about the look on her face when you said you had a tattoo?"

My eyes flashed. "I know. Just as well I didn't mention the belly button ring."

She smiled. "Maybe you can be the trashy unpredictable one at the Darling family get-togethers?"

"I'm sure Adam would love that."

She cocked her head. "He probably would. He's so sprung I'm sure he'd love anything you do."

"I suppose being the wild one would probably be easier than fitting in."

"Totally," she said. "Besides, I always thought not fitting in was kind of your superpower."

"Thanks, Gia. I'm going to take that as a compliment."

"You should," she said. "You're my hero."

"And you're the baddest bitch of honor a girl could ask for."

"Damn straight," she said with a smile. "And don't you forget it."

I raised my glass and clinked it against hers. "Let's get this party started."

FORTY SIX
- Jolie -

The reception had been at peak dance party for hours and showed no signs of abating, so when Adam asked if I wanted to get some fresh air, I jumped at the chance.

"You dance pretty well in that dress," he said, staying between me and the low tide.

"It was tough in the beginning," I said. "But after a few whiskey sours, I didn't notice anymore."

He smiled. "Have I told you lately that I love you?"

"Only in front of all our friends and family, but that doesn't mean I'm sick of hearing it."

"Good," he said.

"Your mom seemed to be having a good time."

He raised his eyebrows. "You told her about your tattoo."

I scrunched my face. "She was shocked, wasn't she?"

"She's from a different generation."

"Gia seems a bit taken with Christophe."

He laughed. "Taken is one word for it. I didn't think our wedding was going to feature that kind of dancing."

"Something for everyone, I guess."

"There was," he said. "You did a great job."

"Thanks," I said, scrunching the damp sand between my toes. "What did you think of the wedding cake?"

"I thought it was delicious. I didn't know you could get cake that was all crushed cookies surrounded by chocolate icing."

"Too rich for you?"

"Not at all. I love to eat a year's worth of sugar in one go. You know that."

I scoffed. "Good thing it was our wedding. A real celebrity probably wouldn't have gone near it."

"Why?"

"Because it's pure fat."

"You should eat more of it then."

I furrowed my brow. "Why? So I balloon?"

"More of you to love," he said, swinging my hand in his.

"If that isn't proof that sometimes the sweet things you say are absolute bull-"

"It's not bull," he said. "I mean it. From now on, I want you to do whatever makes you happy."

"Is that right?"

"Yep," he said. "There's only one condition."

"Which is?"

"I get to be around for it."

"Deal," I said. "In that case, cake for breakfast."

"Make it brunch and you've got a deal."

"Are we going to our spot?" I asked when he turned up the beach.

"Seems only right, doesn't it?"

It wasn't easy trudging through the soft sand in my heavy dress so I was delighted when we finally came to a stop. "God what a crazy day," I said, dropping my hem.

Adam sat right down in his tux and laid on his back.

"What are you doing?"

"It's my party, and I'll lay in the sand if I want to," he said, patting the space beside him before clasping his hands behind his head.

I lowered myself down carefully and leaned back on my elbows.

"You know the first time we came here, you told me to close my eyes and listen to the sea oats."

I smiled. "Yeah."

"It's still my second favorite sound."

"What's your first favorite," I asked. "The ocean?"

He shook his head. "Nope."

"Rain?"

"Nope."

"Dexy's Midnight Runners?"

He laughed. "No. Though I do love some good sax."

"So what is it?" I asked.

"That little moan you do when I-"

I groaned. "I get it."

He smiled at me, clearly amused with himself.

"For such a class act, you sure are filthy."

"It's hard not to be with you around," he said. "So hard."

I laughed and laid back in the sand, folding my hands behind my head. "I guess I better learn to love your filth."

"That's right," he said. "You're stuck with me for good now."

I smiled and let my eyes trace shapes between the stars overhead. "I could've done worse."

He laughed. "Way to big a guy up."

After that we were quiet for a while, just me and the love of my life, listening to the waves and the sea oats as we laid in the sand in our fancy clothes. It was a moment I never could've predicted any more than I ever could've forgotten it.

"I have a confession," he said after a while.

"We need to work on your timing."

"It's about the boat."

I rolled my head towards him.

"It doesn't exactly belong to a friend."

I narrowed my eyes at him. "What does that mean?"

"It means it's my boat."

"What?"

"You heard me."

I shook my head. "Unbelievable."

"Surprise."

I sighed. "You know, a normal person would lie about having a boat and then not have one."

"I guess I got mixed up."

"Why on Earth would you pretend it wasn't yours?" I asked.

"I guess I didn't want you to like me for my big boat," he said. "I'd rather you like me for my big-"

"Very funny," I said. "Why are you telling me this now?"

"Because I had to tell you it was my boat before I tell you this next part."

"I'm listening."

"It's about our honeymoon," he said.

"Go on."

"You know how I said I wanted to take you to the Caribbean?"

I rolled onto my side. "Yeah."

"Well, what I'd really like to do is sail us there."

"Seriously?"

He nodded. "And once we're there, I think we should island hop until we're absolutely positive that we've tried every single cocktail that can be served in a coconut."

"I do like to have a mission."

"So what do you say?" he asked.

"I feel like yes isn't a strong enough word."

"Excellent."

"Wow," I said. "Just when I thought I couldn't possibly look forward to one more thing."

"Married life is great, huh?"

"The best," I said, rolling onto my back again.

A few minutes later, a streak of light zoomed across the sky.

"Oh my god did you see that?" I asked.

"The shooting star?"

I turned my face towards his. "Yeah."

"I did."

"Did you make a wish?" I asked.

"Of course."

"Me too," I said. "Even though it's already come true."

He turned onto his side and propped his head up on his hand. "What did you wish for?"

"I'll tell you if you tell me."

"Deal," he said, fixing his eyes on mine.

I smiled. "I wished for us."

"That's funny," he said. "I wished for you."

Other books in the Soulmates Series

My Best Friend's Brother
A Friends To Lovers Romance

Roommates
A Stepbrother Romance

The Boy Next Door
A Small Town Romance

Made in the USA
Las Vegas, NV
07 January 2023

65149175R00256